Profound passion did not require haste, and each woman thrilled to new and newer heights at the graze of a breast against an arm or the exquisite ache at the beginnings of a new kiss. There was nothing that should be missed in the knowing of each other, nothing to hurry the exploration and the careful tending of so huge a passion.

At the edge of the precipice, even before lips and fingers explored the sweet openings and crevices of love, still there was no hurry. Each separate pang, each separate tremor, demanded its own time and its own life. Finally, one extra spark, a moan, a spasm too many, a breath against an ear broke the dam, and the passion boiled over, steaming and frothing unchecked.

They lay back on the sandy ground. Gilly, far beyond words, felt the errant contractions of spent passion roll on and on in the deepest part of her belly. They lay for a time staring up at the stars and listening to the waves break against the shore. Neither spoke; words were needless in the wake of so magnificent a communion.

MISS PETTIBONE AND MISS McGRAW

by

Brenda Weathers

MISS PETTIBONE AND MISS McGRAW

by

Brenda Weathers

THE NAIAD PRESS, INC.
1995

Printed in the United States of America on acid-free paper
First Edition

Editor: Lisa Epson
Cover designer: Bonnie Liss (Phoenix Graphics)
Typesetter: Sandi Stancil

Library of Congress Cataloging-in-Publication Data

Weathers, Brenda, 1936-
Miss Pettibone and Miss McGraw / by Brenda Weathers.
p. cm.
ISBN 1-56280-151-1
1. Lesbians--Fiction. I. Title.
PS3573.E147M57 1996
813'.54--dc20 95-25557
CIP

For Vicki,
for all these years

About the Author

Brenda Weathers is attempting to grow old gracefully in the wilds of northern New Mexico, enjoying the company of her partner, her dogs, her cats, her geese, and her computer. She is the author of a previous novel, *The House at Pelham Falls* (1986).

The Middle of the Story

One

Gillian Pettibone and Anna McGraw passed into spirit on a chilly autumn evening in the waning years of the 1960s, the sort of evening ready-made for baked apples shared near a blazing hearth or a stroll outdoors under a brilliant canopy of leaves.

It was intended, on that long ago evening, that Gilly alone pass to the next world by consuming an overabundance of capsules, thus ending a lingering and hopeless ailment. On the appointed evening Gilly swallowed a bottleful of bright red pills and, with

Anna cradling her, began in due course to sink into slumber from which her body would not awaken.

Anna watched Gilly's soft passing and knew more heartache and pain than even the months of emotional preparation could have assisted her in withstanding. Just at the moment Gilly eased out her last breath, Anna felt the first searing pain tear into her chest and down her left arm.

Moments later Gilly and Anna were reunited as they hovered together near the ceiling, both staring down at their respective and now useless bodies. Startled, Gilly let out a scream, certain no real sound had come out but just as sure Anna could hear her. Her blessed freedom from pain was a gift most precious. But the shock of seeing Anna hovering right next to her prevented even a cursory investigation of the hereafter.

"What are you doing here?" she demanded, surprised she could talk without the necessity of forming words. It occurred to her that Anna might herself have taken some of the capsules, for they had hoarded more than enough.

Anna smiled, greatly surprised herself, but pleased. What was an aging woman to do anyway, wandering around a big and lonely house for the rest of her days. A gloomy picture indeed, and one that Anna had dreaded from the first moment they knew just how sick Gilly really was. As far as she was concerned, things had worked out just fine. Anna floated nearer to where Gilly hovered, explaining about the sudden pain in her chest and her arrival there on the ceiling.

They huddled next to each other and stared at their discarded remains. Neither expressed the slightest pang of regret. Both were, in fact, feeling better and better about inhabiting the afterlife. They looked with new awe at the pink and yellow flowers hand painted on the globe of the ceiling light. As they tentatively explored their new territory, they saw everything familiar from a slightly different cant, as if reflected through a marred and wavy old mirror.

The afterlife appeared, in fact, to hold a good deal more promise than had their more recent days, weighted down as they were by bodies grown sickly and frail. Perhaps it was in the afterlife, Gilly mused, that life was truly experienced after all, and the before life merely that.

They moved about cautiously, discovering new abilities with such speed that they were scarcely able to understand one before another became obvious. Not only could they talk without using words but they could see through, as well as into, things and began to notice just how colorful they and their surroundings had become. They spent some time in these pleasant discoveries though still did not venture far from the ceiling. There remained, after all, the questions of heaven and hell and the much ballyhooed day of Judgment. Neither had given much thought to matters theological and, in fact, had spent a long and happy life avoiding just such concerns.

"What do you suppose might happen next?" Anna asked cautiously.

"I really couldn't say," Gilly replied while casting her glance outward, beyond the windows and doors. Something of an unpleasant nature might even now be inching toward them. And that something, despite long years of inattention and disregard, might prove harrowing. The prospect of leaving the house loomed as large a fear now as ever — maybe more so, given the circumstances.

Both spirits perceived themselves in a bit of a pickle. To enjoy being bodiless and wafting up by the light fixture was one thing, but to leave the house and its longstanding protection for a menacing encounter at the pearly gates might prove quite another.

They remained still for a long while, contemplating their predicament. It was truly a blessing to find themselves still together in death, but not even the ultimate of life's passages had been forceful enough to overcome their ingrained fear of leaving home.

Since time, as they had known it, was suddenly as useless as the bodies they had left behind, Gilly had no idea how long they had been loitering around the pink and yellow flowers of the ceiling light. "I would have expected something by this time," she said. "Wouldn't you?"

"Yes," Anna said slowly with great deliberation. "That is, if anything is to happen at all. I see no sign of angels or chariots. There's not even a choir."

"Then maybe nothing like that happens at all. The only big differences I notice are the brilliance of color and the lack of need for our worn-out bodies."

Anna grinned, and rather than that being a mere facial gesture, her grin triggered a pleasure for her that ricocheted around the ceiling. "Just the same," she said after a moment, "I think it's best we stay put. We have always been able to count on this house to protect us from the world. Who's to say it won't protect us from the afterworld as well?"

"How right you are," Gilly said and once more

cast about for anything unwelcome. "So far I can't see one frightening thing about having passed over. We can be dead right here in the comforts of our own home."

"Oh, let's," Anna beamed, more thrilled than she could have imagined and immeasurably relieved. As she spoke she began to take on the same golden hue as had Gilly before her.

As usual when a decision had been reached, the matter at hand was considered finished and done with. Tentatively at first, then with growing gusto, Gilly and Anna toured the premises for the first time as spirits, no longer in need of doorways and the like.

It was a large and well built house with a full acre of plum and pear orchards between the house and the road. At the rear of the house a wide, green lawn with brick-circled flower beds swept down to a long, pebbly beach and Puget Sound. The house sat on one of the sprinkling of islands just off the coast of the Northwestern United States, islands that peppered the icy waters of the Sound as though dropped from the pocket of the Creator as She swept northward, pinching off a corner of the Olympic Peninsula and molding the soft curves of British Columbia.

Despite such amenities as these, few visitors ever came to the splendid house, in some measure because of the isolated locale, but primarily because few were invited. Having chosen such an isolated locale Gilly and Anna, for reasons they considered more than valid, vowed seldom to leave its gracious protection.

To reach Plum Tuckered Manor, as Gilly and Anna had christened the place when they first saw it in 1947, the prospective buyers had been obliged to board a ferryboat on the mainland and embark on a cross-Sound trip that required the better part of a day. Thus, there would be little contact with a world that had proven itself narrow, judgmental, and altogether unsuitable for women such as Gilly and Anna, whose lives were nobody's business but their own. Given what had happened to them in the closing days of WWII, they had every right to choose a life of privacy and splendid isolation. When they thought of those horrible events, which was now mercifully seldom, it was to them as if some vulgar, ignorant person had wantonly poured crankcase oil over fine French linen.

The house at the end of the road on a beautiful and very isolated island in the middle of a huge body of water suited Gilly and Anna perfectly. They purchased the property at once. They moved in as quickly as the necessary papers were signed and began exerting their own characters on the old house, which already had much of its own, so that in time it was difficult to tell where one left off and another began.

The house had plenty of windows that let in streams of light and afforded a gorgeous view from each and every one of them. Gilly and Anna filled the place with comfortable overstuffed furniture and a profusion of color in the draperies and slipcovers. They brought in trunk upon trunk of their things, accumulations from years of collecting oddments, souvenirs of their many travels, and personal items of long-standing emotional value. Since both were "savers," this amassed material was joined in short order by carefully wound balls of twine and boxes filled with old magazines and whatever curios from town or tag sales had taken the buyers' fancy.

A couple of music stands, boxes of yellowing sheet music, and several musical instruments, some scattered about in their cases and some hung on walls, decorated the interior. A wicker parrot cage, sans parrot, and a huge pink and blue satin pillow with rose tassels were tucked among the boxes. The pillow had a map of the Philippines on one side and large red letters spelling out Manila on the other.

After a time the house, which couldn't be called dirty, couldn't be called tidy either. "Cleaning is an activity to be exercised with caution," Gilly had warned Anna near the beginning of their relationship. "Especially where 'things' are concerned." Gilly, picking one illustration from many, told Anna about her experience with an oscillating fan in 1937.

The fan was even then an ancient appliance with black blades and a bullet-shaped wire covering. Gilly noticed a thick coating of grime on the blades and set upon the fan with rag and Bon Ami. She scrubbed fervently until the fan looked as if it had been purchased just the day before at Kresge's. When she was done she turned the fan to medium and went quickly on to something more fulfilling.

By midafternoon the fan had begun to emit a strange, gurgling noise. The faithful oscillation became palsied, and by five P.M. the fan hesitated, slowed, then stopped altogether. No amount of well-placed taps or jostling could revive the dead machine. Gilly was obliged to order a new one from the Montgomery Ward catalog since it was summer and Kresge's had sold out.

Anna listened attentively and waited only a short

moment after Gilly was finished with her story to add, "Yes. And the same is true of automobiles, don't you agree? Once you've had them washed, something is certain to break down with the machinery."

"Absolutely. And think for a moment about glass coffee pots. True, if they're not scrubbed they turn a tinge brownish, but the minute you wash one don't you notice how quickly you then accidentally tap it against something and it shatters?"

Everything has its balance, they had concluded, and should be tampered with only minimally—especially inanimate objects in perfect harmony with the natural accretions of time.

Now in this jumble of artifacts, rooms, and crannies, bewildering to the casual observer, but loved in intimate detail by the occupants, would be created both heaven and home. And a more fitting one neither could have imagined.

Due to their erratic and sometimes nonexistent records, and most notably the absence of a will, the house sat empty for quite a long while after their demise. Sooner than they would have liked, however, the state was given its due and the house was placed on the market.

Two

One day, some length of time later, after the FOR SALE sign faded and hung slightly askew on its post, a dust covered sedan turned off the road and into the drive leading to Gilly and Anna's home.

It was a lazy afternoon in midsummer, and Gilly was listening to her beloved Philco. It too had been purchased in 1947 along with the house. She loved the burnished wood and the rounded top and the plastic knobs that looked like caramel. The knobs, while still caramel colored, were no longer necessary.

All Gilly had to do now was give the radio a beam of energy and on it came.

There had been an extremely bleak time after passing to spirit when they had all but given up listening to the radio. The radio worked just fine; there simply was no longer any music to be heard. The twanging, crunching sounds of rock and roll gave them headaches, and even after repeated samplings they usually turned off the radio to sit musing about the fate of lyrics, melody, and the apparent demise of interesting rhythms.

One extremely unpleasant afternoon Anna had beamed at the radio in the narrow hope that something of interest might be playing. The announcer stated, "Stay tuned for more heavy metal!"

"Whatever is that, I wonder?" Anna asked abstractedly.

"Sounds like something one would use to make a garage door," Gilly replied while both waited for the commercial pitch to end.

As soon as the song began, both spirits shot straight upward. Anna beamed the radio off. "How extraordinary!" she exclaimed. "It *was* a garage door."

The radio had been a pleasant but certainly not necessary diversion, for Gilly and Anna knew so many songs that they had often, before dying, exclaimed that it would take an eternity to sing them all.

Sometime later, and by accident, Gilly turned the radio on as she was swept through the room in a particularly good mood. To her surprise she heard Ella Fitzgerald singing "Flying High." A radio station from the mainland was devoting an hour each afternoon to a program of oldies, big band sounds, jazz, blues, and show tunes. Gilly was delighted. Real music!

On the afternoon the car approached the house Gilly was listening intently to Scatman Crothers. The noise of the car drew her attention, however, and she went to the window to look out.

A man got out of a dusty Ford. He was short and pudgy, with a red sausage-like neck. His wife followed a few paces behind, her thin lips already forming around a complaint. The man reminded Gilly of a zucchini that had been left too long in the garden, while his wife, if ever asked to name the animal she most resembled, would have done well to name the ferret.

Anna joined Gilly in the parlor just as the man put a key in the lock and turned it. The man and woman clumped loudly into the entry hall. By this time Gilly had turned the dark sienna of apprehension, and Anna was just behind her in deepening sepia tones.

"I hate it!" the woman shrilled, her voice as sharp as her chin. "That horrible old wallpaper is coming off in chunks. And just look at all that junk!"

"Just hold yer horses," the man countered in a guttural tone. "There's plenty to like about this dump. Startin' with the price." A bitter exchange followed, each combatant vying with the other for supremacy of volume.

Gilly and Anna watched from the other end of the room with mounting horror. They both now glowered a full-blown magenta. The unspeakably rude couple were actually standing in the middle of Gilly and

Anna's own personal heaven! Worse yet, it appeared as if they were there with some intention of buying the place. The man and woman had not stopped disagreeing since setting foot in the door, and the noise of their argument shattered the customary affection and soft silence of Plum Tuckered Manor like breaking crockery.

The man strode noisily across the floor, kicking aside a stack of yellowed sheet music. "Just look at all this junk," he growled. "I'll bet some of this old crap is worth money." Ashes from his cigar fell on the saxophone solo in "One O'Clock Jump."

"Who in the world could have lived here?" the woman shrilled, picking up the satin pillow with the rose-colored tassels and holding it between thumb and forefinger.

"Couple of old biddies," the fat man said and clumped through the French doors to the veranda.

"How dare you touch that pillow," Anna hissed. "Why, if I had a body I'd throw you so far —"

"If you had a body these people wouldn't be here at all, m'dear," Gilly reminded her gently. But for her, too, it was the first time since her demise she had wished for a body. Physical presence, while limited, was at least one way to exert force in certain situations.

Gilly felt scattered and distraught. She cast frantically about looking for something to occupy her, anything to take her awareness away from those awful people. Surely they would leave soon. But meanwhile, she had to do something. They were just too much, those hateful souls. Finally, she hit upon an idea — she would remember something pleasant. She motioned for Anna and, when Anna floated near, put her arm protectively around her shoulder.

"Let's try something." Gilly squeezed Anna's shoulder and told of her plan. To her delight, Anna knew exactly what to do next.

"Let's remember that night, oh, a few years back. We were still in bodies then. I believe it might have been the last time we danced together. Remember?"

"Of course I do. How could I ever forget?" At this, Gilly grinned at Anna, furiously attempting to ignore the muttering, slamming, shouting pair. "Know what?" Gilly took Anna by the hand and led her toward the parlor and the radio. "There is one thing I regret about my life — my afterlife too, for that matter. Only one, mind you. But I do have a regret."

"Whatever is it?"

"That you and I never danced together in public."

Not knowing whether to cry or hug Gilly to her ample bosom, Anna did both. "You old softie," she whispered after a moment. "I never knew that."

"That's because I never told you. If I had, I'm certain you would have taken me to the Empire State building and made me dance with you up there in front of all New York."

"Not a chance, sweetie. I remember what happened in the Philippines as well as you do. But, you know what? I regret that we didn't dance together in public myself. We were so good!"

"Good god!" Gilly exclaimed. "Could you ever cut a rug doing the jitterbug."

Not to be outdone, Anna added laughing, "And no

one has ever done a smoother soft-shoe than you. Not to mention the way we danced the fox trot. Ummm. This takes me back."

"Which brings me back to my point. Let's go back to that day we last danced together. Remember?"

They had been sitting quietly and only half listening to Lawrence Welk. The music wasn't the real thing, of course, but it was a fairly good imitation. In life Gilly was tall and big boned and, since moving to Plum Tuckered, preferred to dress in oversize shirts and sweaters and men's baggy khaki pants. Anna preferred pretty much the same garb, except that on the evening in question she had dragged out an old silk kimono, black with red dragons breathing green fire — another souvenir of the Orient. She was shorter than Gilly and over the years had become quite plump. The kimono was a squeeze, but she was wearing it and, having misplaced the sash, had secured it at the waist with a man's necktie.

Gilly had a cap she was fond of wearing, especially when she was in high spirits. The felt baseball cap, sporting the insignia of the New York Yankees, was mashed down on her graying but still wavy hair.

It had been a perfect day. Fall. They had put up plum butter. Lawrence Welk had just finished one tune featuring the accordion and had eased immediately to the next. Gilly looked at Anna, who was smiling warmly. She stood, with some effort because she was ill but did not yet know it, and walked shakily over to Anna. "Let's dance," she grinned.

Anna, who suffered a painfully arthritic hip, got stiffly to her feet. "My pleasure."

They held on to each other tightly. Gilly led because she was the taller. They limped and shuffled along, but in their minds weak legs and painful hips became miraculously well again. They entered another world where they moved with energy and grace. It wasn't Lawrence Welk but Tommy Dorsey's trombone that played "Begin the Beguine" so beautifully. Now they were dancing in a large ballroom with throngs of others and a spangled silver ball rotating high on the ceiling. On and on they danced and, most miraculous of all in the reassembled version, no one else in the ballroom paid them the slightest notice whatever. They were just another of many young couples in love, swaying to the music and the rarified air of wanting and passion.

When the song ended, Gilly leaned down and kissed Anna softly, just below her earlobe. Anna shivered a little and hugged Gilly tightly against her. "I love you," Gilly whispered.

"Oh, Gilly. And how I love you."

They held onto each other, swaying to music only they could hear. Anna kissed Gilly, first on one closed eye and then on the other. She drew her hand dreamily along Gilly's shoulders and down her spine. Gilly's hands, strong and brown and veined with time, caressed Anna.

They kissed — softly at first then with hunger — and let the stars roll in, each kiss a deep knowing. Each breath, each sigh, each soft gasp spoke a language understood only by them, a language as ancient as time and as fresh as morning. Each knew the other as her very own Velveteen Rabbit, more loved by time and wear than a store full of new dolls. Every contour of their bodies, every line and wrinkle whispered a tale of passion writ large, of life shared together despite overwhelming odds to the contrary.

They moved together toward the stairs leading to their bedroom. As it had been for all time, they were in thrall of each other, their hearts and bodies keening to the bright fire of passion.

It was not without difficulty they climbed the stairs, for each had fallen prey to the afflictions of years, but neither was much aware of their slow progress. The spell was on them. Their spell. No room here for canes or pains. None either for the delusions and disappointments of youth.

Halfway up the stairs Gilly pulled at the tie securing Anna's kimono. It fell open, and Gilly leaned forward to caress Anna's breast, finding as always the soft essence of the woman she had loved so deeply and for so long.

When at last they fell upon the bed it was with the power and abandon of two mighty lovers whose need for each other grew with the ascending steps just as surely as it had with the years.

Apparently this most pleasant reverie succeeded in diverting the ghosts' thoughts from the ruinous pair, but also in turning the man's attention to the Philco. He walked over to the grand old radio and gave it a rough shake. "Wonder if this old relic still works?"

he growled. "This here's a real antique. I bet we could get a lotta money for this thing."

"If you spent half as much time attending your own responsibilities as you do fussing around with other people's junk, we wouldn't have to buy a house like this." The Missus spun on her heel and headed for the kitchen, slamming the door behind her. The Mister followed a few seconds later. "Aw, f'crissakes," he said in a tone that suggested the phrase was easily formed and often used.

Gilly and Anna remained in the parlor, shaken by the rude interruption, yet still glowing a soft rose from the pleasure of the reverie.

After a time, however, the rose glow deepened to a dark magenta as both spirits glared toward the sound of banging cupboards. Gilly had been thinking, and thinking very hard. All of a sudden she turned to Anna. "I can't help but feel we somehow caused that awful man to take an interest in the Philco. Did you notice that he went right to the very object we conjured?"

"Well, yes he did. But better that than the upstairs bedroom," Anna winked.

"Infinitely." Gilly joined in a brief giggle, then again grew serious.

"I think what we think and feel can be noticed by others. I'm not sure, it could be merely a coincidence. But what if it's true?"

"Then lets not waste time, my love. What shall we concentrate on?"

"Certainly not that wonderful night." Gilly beamed Anna a wide, crooked grin. "For this we need something unpleasant. Disturbing."

"Agreed," Anna said, crossing her arms over her chest and staring into the middle distance.

After a small lapse of time, accompanied by an argument in the kitchen, Anna snapped her fingers and beamed. "I've got it. Let's concentrate on that afternoon we played Cleveland. Remember? It was just before we shipped overseas and all the USO guys were drunk. They mobbed us. I didn't think we'd get out alive. That was certainly scary. We could think about that."

"Ummm," Gilly began pacing. "I was thinking more of that gig in Poughkeepsie. We laid an egg, remember? But Cleveland might work just as well. Why conjure too much pain and suffering? God knows, we've got plenty right here. If we just concentrate on how it felt to be frightened and how we wanted to get out of there . . ."

"Well, there's no harm in trying. If Cleveland doesn't work, we'll think of something else. Okay, let's do it." Anna took a seat on the overstuffed sofa and knitted her brow. Gilly joined her, and soon both were enveloped in a thick, streaked haze of purple, blue, and black.

After a time the couple emerged from the kitchen, still arguing. Gilly and Anna stood together in the parlor beaming unpleasantness and fright as hard as they could at a spot just above the couple's eyebrows. The couple remained in the parlor discussing each other's merits, or lack of them, as the ghosts glared.

In time it did seem the Missus became fidgety. She took a hanky from her purse and wiped small beads of sweat from her hairline. Mister appeared unaffected and announced in a booming voice, "We're buying it. And that's that." Missus dabbed at her hairline. "I hate this place," she said, then pursed her lips and narrowed her eyes to indicate Mister would pay for this long after legal instruments had been signed. They headed for the door. "The first thing to go is all this junk," Missus said, sweeping her arm menacingly around the room. "Especially those hideous hydrangeas."

Gilly blanched. She had planted those bushes herself. She had wanted more privacy at the windows and had chosen hydrangeas because they grew quickly and she was partial to large, showy blooms. And there she was, cheek by jowl, in a manner of speaking, with people who wanted everything discarded. Even the plants!

At last the couple left, but Gilly and Anna remained perfectly still, neither wishing to move about in the ugliness left behind. There was no doubt that those small, brittle souls would completely destroy everything. They would harden the gentle atmosphere to the point of breaking. Conceivably, heaven was at an end and the other option was in the offing.

Three

All too soon a pickup truck arrived bearing the Mister and another man. They burst into the house, each carrying an open beer. "Hey man. Look at all this shit. I know people shell out a lotta cash for crap like this," said the other man.

"Me too, me too," Mister replied brusquely. "I'm gonna have somebody make me a bid on the whole lot. But right now, the wife wants this stuff outta here."

"You shoulda paid me more," the other man

whined. "There's a lot more old crap in here than I thought."

"Stop acting like a girl and go out to the truck for a couple more beers, will ya," Mister grumped. "We're heaving this crap out to the barn today, come hell or high water."

It was raining and hell indeed as Gilly and Anna watched the two men carry their belongings ruthlessly to the barn. The spirits peppered the air with exclamations. "Oh, no, not that too." "Be more careful — please." But no matter. The destruction wore on.

Anna turned her back to the men, who were now hauling away their sofa, a cane-backed divan with large, down-stuffed pillows covered in velvet. They had already carried out the matching rocker. Her sadness had been replaced by dark red anger. "Damn it, Gilly. What are we going to do?"

Gilly merely stared at the dismantling of their treasures, her aura the color of wet cement. She shrugged her shoulders and looked as if she might weep. "I feel so helpless," she moaned. "Just like I felt when they tried to arrest us all those years ago. It's so unfair. I hate it." Gilly, too, began glowing dark red around her edges, replacing the concrete hue bit by bit.

Some time later, after the men had left and the house stood empty, they were able to have a reasonable discussion of the matter. The atmosphere had been far too full of the streamlets and shards of colors from the red and orange end of the spectrum.

Later, in a calmer mood, they reasoned that, living as they did in pure essence, furniture and other accoutrements of living might actually prove unnecessary. Perhaps it would be simpler this way. Everything having substance was sure to dwindle, break, and ultimately fade from existence. The human body was a mere example, an inconvenient arrangement at best, requiring food, sleep, and an immeasurable number of consumer goods just to keep it going at all. And in the end, no matter how dedicated the struggle, it gave out anyway. It shouldn't be too difficult, therefore, to make the necessary adjustments concerning their furnishings. They had made plenty of adjustments to the hereafter already, such as never requiring sleep or never having to get organized in the interest of doing things. If necessary, they could just wait it out. After all, they had loads of time.

On a day some while later, a day made more dismal by the events than by the persistent rain, the distasteful couple arrived, accompanied by a truckload of belongings. An argument was underway shortly after the first cartons were carried into the house. Arguing continued unabated throughout the day, and while the subject might differ from time to time the underlying tone of hostility did not. Missus would like the paper towels to hang from the back of the roll while Mister preferred they hang more accessibly at the front. He wanted the bath mat placed over the shower rod when not in use, while she preferred it hung over the side of the tub. As each new conflict arose, each presented the merits of their arguments and marshaled them as evidence of the general failings in judgment and character of the other.

After a day of unceasing disagreement and

nastiness so pervasive Anna feared it might actually materialize, the pair wafted among the half-emptied cartons and heaps of other people's minutiae in pale hues. Gilly was silent, contemplating her diminished aura. "I just can't take it," she said at last. "I mean it, Anna. It's not so much the loss of our things as it is the proximity to these horrible people. It simply won't do."

"I know, sweet," said Anna. "I feel the same. But I don't see any alternatives." In an attempt at levity, she added with a grin, "Certainly suicide is out of the question."

Gilly began an aimless roaming of the disarray within their home and Anna followed, both deep in concentration. They wandered the whole house, except for the upstairs bedroom where the intrusive pair were fast asleep and snoring. Eventually they wandered into the kitchen and wafted there, quietly looking around. Gilly's attention fell on a sizable row of beer bottles with differing amounts of fluid in each. Mister had been drinking from them all afternoon, which had only served to make him more bellicose. She concentrated on the collection of bottles so long and hard that Anna's attention was drawn to them as well. "I never cared much for beer," was all Anna could think to say. "As I recall, neither did you."

"No, I much preferred a good gimlet, or a Rob Roy, or even a martini, but with onion, no olives." Gilly said this almost absentmindedly, as one does when forced into conversation while thinking of something else.

"Why ever are you staring at those beer bottles,

Gilly?" Anna asked after a while. "Your concentration is so intense that I'm forced to pay attention myself. And frankly, I don't see the attraction."

It seemed they were on the verge of an argument themselves. Something in the befouled air had doubtless rubbed off.

Gilly disentangled herself from the bottles. "Just let me think a minute," she said with apology. She turned to face Anna. "What if," she said slowly and with great deliberation, "what if we could scare them away."

"Oh, pooh!" Anna replied, a little stunned. "You know I want those people out of here as badly as you do. But, frankly, we're hardly frightening specimens. I just can't imagine us —"

Gilly's color was brightening from magenta to a much softer, more humorous flamingo. "Just listen, Anna. Ghosts scare people. It's a fact of the hereafter. Think of all the Poe you've read, or the Henry James."

Picturing clanking chains and musty shrouds, Anna looked at Gilly, "Oh, I don't —"

"Look over there." Gilly pointed at the parade of beer bottles. "When you were a child, remember making odd noises, sometimes even songs, by blowing over the tops of bottles? There must be fifteen bottles over there, each with a differing level of liquid. The tonal possibilities are endless."

Anna brightened. She moved over to the bottles, stared at them, then looked at Gilly and exclaimed, "Why, there are enough notes here to play any number of songs. Right now I can see the possibilities for 'Don't Sit Under the Apple Tree.' Not all the notes are there, but at least we'll know what we're playing."

In less than the bat of an eye, they lined up straight as an arrow in front of the bottles and bent down. They concentrated their ethereal energy over the tops of the bottles, as one would blow air from a windpipe. Within moments they had worked through the first few bars of one of their old favorites.

"Oh, this is delicious, Gilly. We just wait until they're asleep, then come in here and make a whale of a racket. Honestly, you're a genius."

"That's exactly it, Anna," Gilly said after smiling and casting her eyes to the floor, as she always did when Anna paid her a compliment. "Only let's think of it more as a haunting melody, shall we?"

They fell against each other and went all through the house laughing and stumbling and hooting. They laughed so hard that if they'd had functioning tear ducts they would have needed a whole box of tissues. At one point, Anna lay down and, holding her midsection, kicked her legs up and down on the bare floor. Gilly leaned against a box of cartons, weak and helpless to stop laughing.

After they had laughed themselves and the house into a sparkling vermilion, they returned, exhausted, to the kitchen. "Actually, why should we wait?" said Anna. "They're asleep. There's nothing to stop us from playing them a little tune."

"Nothing at all," Gilly chortled. "Let's focus our energy and concentrate very hard. I think we'll have to play much louder this time." They readied themselves over the bottles, and after a practice toot or two Gilly said, "Hit it."

Unfortunately, even with the B-flat missing, "Don't Sit Under the Apple Tree" sounded far from frightening. Soon they gave up the pursuit of melody in favor of odd toots and discordant rills. They huffed and puffed away, but to their utter disappointment, no noise of awaking, much less screaming, sleepers could be heard in the upstairs bedroom. "I'll just go up there and have a look-see," volunteered Anna. "Maybe they are awake and scared out of their wits but too frightened even to jostle the bed clothing and get up."

"Good idea. I'll stay here and step up the tempo."

Anna returned a short time later and reported that neither of the sleepers appeared to have suffered the slightest disturbance. "What needs stepping up is the volume, not the tempo," Gilly mused. "But I'll be a purple cow if I can think of a way."

"I think we're just too scattered this evening," Anna offered. "Just think of all the emotions we've run through today. We need to spend our time quietly, gathering back all the disjointed points of energy we've left scattered about. After all, there'll be another night tomorrow. We have all the time in the world, as they say."

The following day was much the same as the day before, most of it devoted to depressing arguments. Gilly and Anna focused themselves with determination and made veritable islands of calm in the surrounding storm. Mister drank a lot of beer and became quite drunk. He retired early while Missus sat up plotting her various revenges. Finally she too went to bed, and soon after Gilly and Anna stationed themselves once again before a row of bottles on the kitchen counter.

The tooting began and, just as Anna had suggested, with considerably more volume. Sure enough, this time they heard muffled rumblings and rustlings in the upstairs bedroom. Both ghosts stopped blowing and sped up the staircase to have a look. Both the woman and the man appeared to be sleeping, although their covers were a jumble as though they had spent a somewhat fitful period. Heartened by their modest success, Gilly went down to the kitchen to toot some more, asking that Anna remain at the bedside to take note of any effects.

In a few moments, as Anna peered down on the sleepers, Gilly began a vigorous blowing across the bottles.

"Wha' was that?" the woman sputtered, sitting bolt upright in bed. She nudged Mister in the ribs. He turned on his side and made a pretense of listening. Muttering something about calling a plumber, he quickly fell back to sleep. The Missus sat up a while longer, looking warily about and cocking her head in the direction of the kitchen, before she, too, fell back asleep. Gilly continued tooting, but no amount of effort awakened the snoring couple again that night.

Not to be deterred, Gilly and Anna continued the nightly tooting. Missus now awoke every night, but instead of vowing to leave the house by morning's first light — as both Gilly and Anna hoped — she merely pulled the bedclothes to her chin and darted her eyes about the room. She lost sleep and appeared the worse for it. Her daily confrontations with Mister were more animated and even more liberally peppered with her shrill, "I hate this place."

"I don't know, Anna," Gilly said one evening after

a particularly raucous concert during which the Missus had once again sat up wide-eyed and wary. "We aren't exactly shooing them out of here. I feel a little depressed. It isn't like us to fail at something."

"Then I'm sure we haven't. We'll think of a way. We always do." Gilly cast her eye about the room. How peaceful it had all been when only she and Anna had the run of the place. Gilly continued her examination of the parlor, taking in the gold brocade sectional sofa with clear plastic covering, the coffee and occasional tables made from laminated plastic. Everything was so sterile. Nothing blended with anything else. Nothing was in the least compatible with, and certainly not forgiving of, the character and boundaries of the thing next to it. A hodgepodge of rigidity and discomfiture.

On a small table near the door where the couple had installed a telephone, Gilly now noticed a small but compelling incongruity. On the table sat a vase of bright yellow daffodils, left the day before by the Welcome Wagon lady. Gilly stared at the soft yellow petals with the white center, admiring the beauty and happy reappearance of fresh flowers in the house. The longer she stared, the more insistent the sensation that something important perched on the brink of unfolding.

When Gilly's notion came to full bloom, she jerked to an upright position and swirled to face Anna. "The flowers," she said. "The flowers."

"Yes. Lovely, aren't they? It's so nice to have flowers around again."

"Yes, yes. But that's not what I'm talking about. Look at how they shine. They're like us. Don't you see? There's a halo around them. Kind of a radiance."

"True."

"Picture this. What if we could borrow some of that radiance? If we could borrow enough, then maybe we could — what do you call it? — materialize."

"Now, wouldn't that be the berries," Anna said, seizing the possibilities at once. "We could borrow the radiance, then hurry upstairs and whoosh around at the foot of their bed. Oh, how perfect. Surely that will frighten them silly. Imagine seeing two old ladies, glowing slightly yellow, swaying and swirling just inches off the floor. I'd leave. And that's a fact."

"No doubt," Gilly laughed. "But on second thought, perhaps only one of us should try to materialize, as there's precious little radiance in those flowers as it is. There might not be enough to go around."

"Right you are. You borrow the radiance. But be sure to return any that's left over. Meanwhile, I'll blow over the bottles as before."

The following evening, spirits high, Gilly wafted against the flowers, vastly relieved they hadn't been tossed out during the day. She began drawing in energy, inhaling, so to speak, and sure enough a bright yellow tinge began to outline the shape of her. Thrilled and fascinated, she watched as her coloration became more pronounced. "Run upstairs quick, Gilly," Anna yelled. "The flowers are looking pale and rather sickly." With that, Gilly took a deep draft and sped for the stairway. Anna ran for the kitchen and began blowing.

Although Anna was outdoing herself, the couple

didn't stir as Gilly entered the bedroom. Gilly sailed to the foot of the bed, dismayed that her bright yellow tint had already faded a bit. *Blow harder,* she thought to Anna.

At last the couple stirred. Gilly screwed her face into a grimace. Anna tooted. Just then Missus awoke and sat up in bed. Her eyes grew large with fear and she screamed, "Yieee." At that point, Mister awoke. He, too, saw Gilly's swirling yellow form and the ill will in her grimace. He sat upright, bolted out of bed, and scrambled downstairs and out of the house, leaving his wife to contend with the apparition. Missus threw her wrapper over her shoulders and followed her husband into the night. A car started and sped out of the driveway.

Four

Shortly following the late-night departure of the unpleasant pair, afterlife at Plum Tuckered Manor returned pretty much to normal. No mortal inhabitants were about the place, and once again Gilly and Anna returned to their usual routines.

Picking up the pieces was preoccupying and pleasant; both Gilly and Anna exuded an aura of triumph at their overwhelming success. Soon the nasty interlude was hardly spoken of at all.

There was an all but palpable twinkling and a rich rosy aura once again in the house. One afternoon they stood quite close to one another and gazed out across the lawn to the water. Relief and joy had led to a certain mischievousness, and it was in this mood that Anna grinned at Gilly and said, "You know, we learned something from those two. Well, not from them so much as from what happened."

"What, for heaven's sakes?" For all her inventiveness and courage, Gilly could sometimes be irritatingly pragmatic.

"Well, remember when you borrowed the radiance from those flowers?"

"Yes. Wasn't it grand? And when I gave back the borrowed radiance, remember how great the flowers looked? Much better than before we began tampering with them."

"Yes, that's all true," Anna grinned wider. "But actually, I'm getting at something else."

Gilly studied the colors around Anna for a sign of her meaning. "Go on," she urged.

"Well what goes up, must come down." Anna proceeded slowly, but with a definite tone of self-satisfaction. "There is an up and a down to everything. Up, down. Black, white. Yin, yang. Balance is everything in the laws of nature."

Gilly began pacing, growing impatient. Sensing this, Anna rushed on. "See, if you could remove something from flowers, perhaps it's also possible to put something into them, or into anything. Say, something like yourself."

"Good heavens, Anna. Do you know what you're saying?"

"Well, not every detail, of course. But basically, I'd be willing to bet something like that would be possible."

Both spirits contemplated the possibilities, as well as the drawbacks, in silence. Experiencing one's own realities can be difficult enough. What of the difficulties encountered when experiencing the realities of another?

"We pass through things all the time," Anna said after a time of silence, "doors, walls, the like. Don't you think it might be possible to merely stop, instead of just wafting through?" Anna paused for a moment and looked at Gilly, "More or less like applying the brakes."

"You're suggesting we sidle up to anything we choose and enter it? It's a delicious idea. And we might actually have quite a time of it." Even though Gilly felt those things to be true, still she felt a certain hesitation. Her glance fell on a philodendron left behind by the departing couple. It had not had water for who knew how long and had begun to turn a brittle, brownish color at the edges. She eased nearer the plant, experiencing an admiration for its tenacity. What if philodendrons hate Bach's Fugue in G Minor but are committed to hear the particular piece of music due to the taxonomically higher species with access to the dials? Worse, what if she entered the philodendron but couldn't get back out again. She should be forced to spend a possibly lengthy time crowded up inside a wilting and browning plant.

"What if we couldn't get out again?" she blurted.

"I've been thinking about that, too," Anna replied.

"But I feel certain everything will work out. Think of it more as 'visiting.' When we're ready to leave, we just move on, take off the brake."

Gilly liked the notion. It probably was a simple enough thing to do, and she was surprised neither of them had thought of it before. But necessity truly is the mother of invention and, had it not been for the couple, they would never have needed to explore those realms.

"I think you're entirely right, Anna. It'll be a breeze. Only let me go in first. I'm feeling exceptionally sturdy today."

"Sure, if you want to. But as quickly as you're back, I'm next. And if you don't come back, I'll devote my eternity to sitting beside you singing 'Mountain Greenery.' "

"Very funny," Gilly said and moved closer to the plant. "Well, here goes." She moved even closer, more or less directing herself into the space between the molecules along one wilted frond.

Anna watched Gilly disappear entirely into the plant. The philodendron looked exactly the same even, with Gilly inside. She wasn't worried in the least about Gilly; she knew it would be all right. She did feel a bit of impatience, as she wanted to fling herself into the plant as soon as possible.

Not a long while later Gilly emerged, looking triumphant but a touch pale.

"How was it?"

"Interesting," she replied, making a face as if she were about to sneeze. "But I found photosynthesis rather ticklish. And it had a sooty taste, like Earl Grey tea. I never cared much for Earl Grey tea."

Anna, who had a penchant for Earl Grey tea,

leapt into the plant in the flutter of an eye. She, too, emerged without incident a short time later. The atmosphere in the room became jubilant. Whole new vistas had been opened.

On an afternoon a time or so later, Gilly looked out the window and saw a large gray tabby stalking an insect on the lawn. The cat obviously belonged to someone, for it was sleek and fat and it often came to play among the fascinations of the overgrown yard and orchard. Both found great amusement in watching the cat go about her pleasures. They felt certain the cat knew they were there watching as she played. Sometimes, after a particularly stunning leap and pirouette, the cat would pause and turn toward the house. With a self-satisfied look, the cat would then stare at the window, preening for a long moment before stalking off in search of new admirers.

"Wouldn't it be fun," Gilly suggested, "to find out what it's really like to be a cat."

"I've always imagined it would be the most luxurious of feelings," Anna offered. "Like living endlessly in a mouton coat — without becoming too warm, of course."

The cat remained perfectly still while the ghosts considered the ramifications of becoming it. "We've never gone into anything alive before," Anna pointed out.

"Of course we have. Think of the plant. Besides, there's life in everything. Even us. Rocks, trees, cats. Everything gives off color, and disturbs the air with waves of energy. Still, I see your point. We've never entered something that might possibly react."

"Hmmm, yes. I imagine it would create quite a start to all of a sudden have another being bumping around inside one's body. But what if the cat is asleep at the time?"

"Well now, that might work. Except cats are known to be very light sleepers."

"Not that gray tabby. I've seen that old cat sleep for hours sunning herself in the orchard."

"Did you see where she went?"

"No. But she'll show up. She always does."

"Good. Then let's just wait a while. After she's played a bit she'll require a nap. We can flip a coin to see who gets to try it first."

"And if there is any unhappy disturbance to the cat we will stop immediately, okay?"

"Well, of course. Certainly. It's impossible to be cruel to someone whose legs end with paws."

Not too long a while later, the cat appeared and began stalking something in the tall grass. True to form, she played a while before settling herself carefully in a puddle of sunshine for an afternoon snooze. Gilly reassembled from memory a shiny quarter and tossed it into the air. Both bent to watch the coin spin on the floor. "Heads!" Anna cried. "That's me."

She was outside in a flash and inching her way toward the unsuspecting animal. After only the slightest hesitation she inched her way alongside the rich thick fur, parted it, and eased her way inside. Once inside, Anna focused on the luxuriousness she experienced there, the sinewy power. She felt compelled to move about in such extraordinary circumstances. Oh, the lightness of it! The acute awareness!

Hoping not to awaken the cat she stretched one paw and, before she could stop herself, leaned forward and licked the fur on her right leg with her emery-board tongue. Immense satisfaction filled her and came out her throat. So much fur, so soft. She had to stretch. She thrust her back high in the air and made her head and forepaws level to the ground. Wonderful! She dug her claws into the grass, muscles taut. A moth was in the foreground. *I can see every mote of dust on the wings. Be still, don't make a move. The moth is my universe. It shimmers in light. Be still. Be the moment. Be the precise moment. Now!*

Effortlessly soaring high, forepaws extended. Swat! Down easy. Open mouth. Drop moth. Watch. Be the moment. In the moment. Go! Paw. Lightning fast. Moth. Bite.

I could do this forever, Anna thought. And she realized that, much more than merely being inside the cat, she was becoming the cat. Anna struggled to separate her own consciousness from that of the cat. Nevertheless, she simply had to swoop the moth up with her paw and examine it closely. She arched her back and trotted closer to the house, where she dropped the dead moth on the grass so that Gilly might enjoy it as well. She sat on her haunches beside it, perfectly balanced and perfectly still. She turned her head slowly to the side so that onlookers might be afforded a profile. She could see Gilly very clearly through the window. Gilly smiled and waved, wriggling her fingers in the air.

Just at that moment Anna felt a slight jerk that she had not caused. And something else was happening, too. Another consciousness was awakening just beside hers. *The cat is waking up,* she thought. *I must get out. Now!* With that she eased herself slowly out of the slightly dazed animal.

Anna wafted quickly into the house to stand beside Gilly at the window. "It's indescribable," was all she could say. They both turned to look at the cat.

The tabby looked as bewildered as Gilly and Anna were ecstatic. She crept close to the ground at the place where she had awakened and sniffed the grass, looked with amazement at the fallen moth, then stared at the place next to the tree where she had originally fallen asleep. Her tail switched quickly back and forth.

"Poor thing. She's so confused," said Anna. "In the future, we must be sure to put everything back where we found it."

Thus began an exhilarating time at the Manor. The spirits whooshed in and out of objects both animate and otherwise and were often away from the house for prolonged periods. One day they arrived at the house, having just had the exquisite pleasure of finding two sleeping cats and cavorting together in the orchard, and were unpleasantly surprised to find someone was there.

A ladder was propped against one wall in the bare room, and a man dressed in white coveralls was stirring a can of paint. He whistled to himself and seemed, on the whole, quite mild. "I had a feeling something like this was going to happen," Gilly said.

"Something like what? What is happening?"

"Do you remember that day we were out playing with the otters? Well, when we came back in I remember having the distinct feeling that someone had been here."

"Really? Like who?"

"That I don't know. All I can say is that whoever it was left no unpleasant feeling behind. In fact, nothing seemed in the least disturbed. I'd quite forgotten about it until just now."

"I'll bet I know what's happening then," Anna said. "Someone else has bought the place. They're having it painted. Someone else is moving in here!" Alarm sounded in her voice.

"Yes, but maybe it won't be so bad this time," Gilly offered. "Maybe we'll get lucky, and some sweet little old lady with hundreds of cats and no one to argue with will buy the place."

"That would be nice, wouldn't it?"

At that moment the painter turned on a portable radio he had brought with him. After some static and fiddling with the knobs, the radio blared out at full volume "Chattanooga Choo Choo."

"Oh, how that takes me back," Gilly said.

"Me, too. And you know what, Gilly? Those were wonderful times really. We had such fun. Even with everything that happened later."

"True, Anna. So very true." Gilly was beginning to glitter.

"Hey, how about it, Anna. Once more for old time's sake. Let's jump in on this one."

In an instant it was 1944 again. In a huge ballroom, with a silver revolving ball in the ceiling, Gilly and Anna faced the audience. They wore matching sequined gowns and each stood before a large microphone. Beyond the mike a large audience of dancers and listeners swayed to the music. On cue, they faced stage left, turned their faces, and extended right arms to the audience and belted in perfect harmony, "You'll leave the Pennsylvania Station 'bout a quarter to four . . ."

The Beginning of the Story

Five

The noon train sat on the track at Grand Central Station, steam belching from the engine and hissing along the tracks. As the wheels of engine number 9 began a slow, rumbling roll, the conductor leaned out and yelled, "All abooo-ard."

Gillian Pettibone raced through the crowded terminal, almost colliding with a smartly dressed Army corporal. " 'Scuse me," she mumbled and righted herself. She spread a wide apologetic smile over her face. "It's just that I'm so —"

"So late." He finished and tipped his hat. "Everybody's late these days. With the war on —"

"So true," she said and, without waiting for him to finish, smiled and turned away, dashing through the throngs in the terminal.

By the time Gillian reached the train it had already gathered a little steam and was moving slowly down the track. She grabbed for the handle of her coach as it rolled past. With the help of a handily placed porter, she threw two of her bags into the gangway, clutched the third, and hauled herself onto the train.

She stowed the two bags in a rack in the coach compartment and climbed the short flight of steps to the passenger compartment. Hers was an aisle seat and the only vacant one in the entire car. She flopped down with a large sigh next to a very fat man whose beefy arms commanded both the armrests. He took a puff from a thick cigar.

Gillian struggled with her other bag, a black leatherette instrument case, trying to position it so that it fit under her seat. She pushed and prodded until the leatherette case covered with bright decals of her travels rested evenly on the floor. She propped her feet on the part that stuck out under her seat and let out a sigh.

As soon as she settled comfortably into her chair the fat man turned to her. "Say, kiddo. Going all the way to Chi Town?"

Gillian curled her bottom lip and expelled another breath so that the force of it parted her bangs. "Yes." She said this as simply and matter of factly as possible to discourage further talk. Conversation with anyone, especially the man next to her, was the last thing she needed. She was tired, rumpled and, as of this moment, entirely mad as hell.

She looked down at her clothing and found her new outfit already wrinkled and sooty. Actually, it came as no surprise to her that she seemed to exist in a state of perpetual though mild disarray. But, my god, it was only a little after noon. That morning she had carefully dressed in a medium red gabardine suit with slacks that were pleated at the waist and a matching jacket with wide, padded shoulders. She had bought a beige rayon blouse to wear with it and soft beige wedgies with red leather trim. Gillian loved the jauntiness of her new suit, and she especially loved wearing a good pair of trousers. She liked to saunter about in them, hands jammed into the deep side pockets, or walk in long, meaningful strides and feel the trouser material flutter at her ankles. She was learning, in fact, what men had known for ages — that wearing pants somehow gave one a bigger sense of freedom, a heightened feeling of mobility in the world. As a consequence, she had worn nothing but trousers since signing up with the USO over a year and a half ago.

The fat man, not easily dissuaded by his companion's short reply, extended his hand so that it stuck out in the air just over her lap. "Name is Mead," he said. "Say, what's that you're carrying?"

"My saxophone," she said with premeditated distance.

"Well, whaddya know. I used to play a little sax myself. Never got to be very good, though. My father used to raise hell every time I tried to practice. Said it made his teeth shiver. Ha ha." The man looked more closely at Gillian. "So. You're musical, too. It's kinda odd to see a lady saxophone player, but, with the war on and all, everything is purty much topsy-turvy. Me, I'm 4F. Say, where do you play?"

Gillian sighed. "I'm with the USO. We play clubs all over the country, for the troops."

"Are there any other girls in the band?"

"We're all girls. Everybody in the band is a girl."

"Well, don't that take the cake." The man let go with a rumpled laugh. "What's the name of your group?"

"The Musi-Gals."

"Well, ain't that the cutest thing I ever heard."

Gillian wanted to strangle him. She was not in the mood for conversation. To make matters worse, she was definitely getting a screamer of a headache. Ever since this morning at the USO office, things had not gone her way.

She had gotten up and gone to the office early to sign a mound of chits and itinerary papers, but in the midst of the task her boss, Nolan Phelps, walked in and stood behind her. Just the situation she had wanted to avoid. He cleared his throat, and she turned around. "Well," he said primly, taking off his spectacles and wiping them with a pressed hanky. "You're just the lady I needed to see this morning. Seems we have a bit of a problem."

Gillian didn't like his tone in the least. She didn't like it almost as much as she didn't like Phelps himself. The feeling, she knew, was mutual. Phelps hadn't been able to get into the service because of his stature and weak eyes and, feeling he should have been at least accepted for some high-level intelligence post, felt threatened by almost anyone having contact with the war — especially if that person happened to be female. She whirled around.

Gillian rather enjoyed standing taller than Nolan. She towered over him. He stood at five four while she tallied in at five eight. She thrust her hands into her trouser pockets, glad for the little extra height the wedgies gave her. Nolan looked up at her with the hateful little smirk that passed for a smile. "Seems our Della won't be going along to Chicago with the band." He put his spectacles back on his nose and almost snorted.

"Why not?" Gillian asked, some color already rising to her cheeks.

"Well, just the usual, I guess."

Gillian glared at him. "Out with it, Nolan. It's too early in my day for coy business managers."

"I'm not being coy, my dear, just stating the facts."

"Then state some!"

Phelps seemed eager to oblige. "Seems our Della has run off with some sailor from Nebraska. She says they're getting married over in Jersey before the bridegroom ships out for Okinawa. How do you like that?" He paused for emphasis. "One minute Della's singing with the band. The next she's holed up in a motel room in Jersey making whoopee."

Nolan walked to his desk and sat down. "Just like I always say: Women aren't right for this line of work. You should all be home making babies."

Gillian bit her lip and stormed to a grimy window that looked down on 42nd Street. She didn't know whom to be madder at, Della or that weasel Phelps.

He had it in for her, she knew that, but then he had it in for all women. More than once he had complained up the chain of command that the bands playing their clubs should be male only. Women were just too much trouble.

Christ, what a fine mess. Gillian struggled to get her temper and her breathing under control. *Good god. Now what will the band do?* The gigs in Chicago were all lined up, as were the musical numbers. Della and Gillian were the featured vocalists. They had only just finished a frolicking arrangement of "Chattanooga Choo Choo" that was to be the grand finale of the band's set. Gillian was the bandleader and the saxophonist, but she also doubled as the alto voice on the vocal numbers. She and Della, in fact, had liked to think of themselves as the Andrew Sisters minus one. But who the hell wants to hear an alto singing alone?

After she had composed herself, Gillian strode to Nolan's desk and, spreading her long hands out on the gleaming surface, leaned toward him. "We have to do something, Nolan. Something more constructive than you sitting behind this desk and gloating."

"I've already thought of that," he said, again taking off his spectacles. He began rummaging through a pile of papers. "When I heard about Della yesterday, I had the front office wire bios of some recent applicants. I think I have the perfect person. Actually, she's all we could do on such short notice." He pulled a piece of paper from the stack, replaced his glasses, and stared up into Gillian's glowering face. "Here, you want to read this?" he asked and slid the paper toward her.

"No, you tell me about it, okay, Nolan? I mean,

the decision has obviously been made. Why should I have anything to say about it?"

"Have it your way," he said.

"I'll try," Gillian retorted through set lips.

"Lucky for you we just happened to have a bio on a girl singer from St. Louis. She's anxious to do something for the cause and writes that she's had professional singing lessons and has appeared at local musical functions."

Gillian groaned. *Dear god, not some hayseed whose only experience is performing at ice-cream socials and barn dances. Please.*

Willing her face to betray nothing, Gillian asked calmly, "So, does she say what kind of music she sings or for how long?"

"Here, let me take a look." Nolan made a pretense of studying the page. After an agonizing time he looked up smiling. "*Opera,* it says here. Yes. Opera."

Gillian thought her knees would buckle. "Opera!" *Oh, my god! Damn Della! Damn Nolan! Damn everything!*

She glanced at the clock, a huge black Regulator, and realized that if she stayed much longer she was sure to miss her train. Words came tumbling out in a torrent. "Surely you can't expect me to go on the road with a girl who only sings opera and hasn't a jaybird's chance of learning swing or bebop and who will embarrass us all. And in front of all those people." The more Gillian talked, the higher her voice got. "Damn it, Nolan. Get me somebody else."

"No can do, kiddo. She's all there is, and she's already on the Midwest Flyer, figuring to meet up with you and the gals in Chi Town."

"Damn!" Gillian muttered.

She looked again at the time and knew she had to dash right that minute. As it was, she would just make it. She swooped the necessary papers into her bag and looked directly into Nolan's pinched face. More than anything she wanted to bloody his nose. She screwed up her mouth to say something, but all that came out was a sputter. She turned and stalked to the door, allowing it to slam resoundingly at her departing back.

She sat on the train inching through a seemingly endless jungle of factories and warehouses, her head aching and her mind racing at full tilt. She felt certain the fat man was going to talk to her again, so she let her head roll to one side and closed her eyes. Sleep, however, was the last thing she expected. There was far too much to think about, to do, in the wake of Della's traitorous departure. She wondered where the rest of the girls were, and how in god's name she could break the news. Images of a singerless swing band and a ballroom full of yawning people swam before her eyes.

Vaguely she heard the fat man talking, more or less to himself, and felt herself begin to doze. She had gotten up awfully early that morning and maybe just a little snooze . . .

The next thing Gillian knew someone was shaking her shoulder. "Reveille, Pettibone. Up and at 'em."

Missy, the band's drummer, peered at her. "Hey," she said, "whatcha doin' way up here. We're all back in the club car. C'mon sleepyhead. You're missing all the fun."

Sleepily Gillian rose, grabbed her saxophone, and followed Missy to the lounge car. The girls were there all right. She counted everyone as she entered, smiling and waving as if everything were just peachy. "Hi, everybody," she called and plopped down at a small table between Marge, the lead trumpet, and Lil, the bass fiddle. A number of gin and tonics were already on the table. The barman appeared, and Gillian ordered coffee and a grilled cheese sandwich. It was much too early to start sipping gin.

Missy pulled up a chair and joined them. She took a sip of her fresh drink and leaned toward Gillian. "How 'bout that Della, huh?" Missy's eyes were lively, showing equal measures of concern and expectation of good gossip.

"You mean you already know?" Gillian took a scalding sip of her coffee and set the cup down.

"Oh, sure, honey. Carolyn found out from this guy she sometimes sees when we're in the Big Apple. He's a clerk in Phelp's office. Anyway, he told Carolyn all about Della and her fella — gee, I made a poem," Missy laughed and continued. "But before we get into the juicy stuff, what the hell is the band going to do without a singer?"

Gillian stared at her untasted grilled cheese sandwich. "We have a singer," she replied flatly.

"We do?" everyone exclaimed at once. Gillian looked at the circle of very round eyes, swallowed hard, and said, "Phelps has already assigned somebody. She's even at this minute on the Midwest

Flyer, hurtling toward us." A chorus of questions filled the car.

Gillian stood and spread her hands in mock supplication. "Okay. Just everybody listen up a minute." Sotto voce, she asked Missy if everybody in the band knew.

"Sure they do, dummy. Do you think a piece of news like that would stay hush-hush around here? Just look around. Everybody is practically falling out of her seat and I don't mean from gin."

Gillian looked around the car. Sure enough, seven pairs of anxious eyes were riveted on her. Well, they had to find out sooner or later. Guess it might as well be sooner.

"So who is she?" Lil asked for the group. "Has she got any experience?"

"Look, I don't know a whole lot more than you do." Gillian made a special effort to steady her voice and project calm. After all, if she flipped her wig, then so would everybody else. "Everybody just try to relax, and I'll tell you what little I know."

She struggled for the right words and finding none blurted out, "She sings opera." A heavy silence fell over the club car.

Missy took another long pull on her gin and tonic as did Lil. Marge stopped eating a handful of peanuts in mid-chew. Each woman stared at Gillian with looks ranging from the incredulous to Lil's bemused half smile.

"Opera!" someone blurted. Then, except for the low moan of the train's whistle and tinkle of glassware from the bar, the car was silent.

No one spoke, each woman contemplating the news. Finally Betse, who played trombone at least as sweet as Jimmy Dorsey, sang out, "I wonder if you can sing scat to Verdi?"

Everybody laughed, even Gillian. She laughed until tears streamed down her cheeks because, admit it, the picture of some big bosomed, blonde Valkyrie in a horned helmet trying to sing scat like Ella was a hilarious sight indeed. An opera singer on tour with a swing band! What next! After several moments of hilarity, Gillian snapped into a fully erect posture and again grew somber. She pushed aside the grilled cheese sandwich, for which she hadn't the slightest appetite, and folded her hands precisely on the table. "All right, listen up. We've got work to do."

"Not so fast, Pettibone," Missy said. "Give us the scoop. When do we meet her? What's her name?"

Gillian fumbled through papers and withdrew one from her bag. "Just a minute, I'll have to look. I don't know myself." Finally, grasping the bio sheet in one hand, she read. "It's McGraw. Anna McGraw."

Later, after most of the others had gone to catch an afternoon nap, Missy asked, "So, Pettibone. What are you going to do? We're scheduled for two weeks in Chicago starting tomorrow night, and I'd sure as hell hate to see us make fools of ourselves. Maybe we should drop all the duet numbers and add some Cole Porter."

"Exactly what I was thinking. We'll need a long rehearsal as soon as we hit the hotel, but maybe we can get some numbers together in time. Phelps can make us take her, but he sure as hell can't make us put her in front of a microphone. I only regret I have to wake up in the middle of the night to meet her at the station." Gillian yawned and rested her head against the scratchy seat.

* * * * *

She awoke sometime later to someone jostling her shoulder. "Wake up, Miss Pettibone. We're pulling into the station. You wanted to be awakened." Gillian looked up into the porter's face and tried to shake herself awake. She could not remember feeling so tired, nor so sore from sleeping cramped up in the train's hard seat. She checked her watch. It was ten minutes to midnight. With a groan she pushed herself out of the seat and realized she was not only sleepy and sore, but still in a very bad mood.

Sleepily Gillian made her way through the darkened coach and down the steps to the platform. Outside, the night was cold. A stiff wind assaulted her and blew a discarded newspaper across the platform. While the wind and cold invigorated her a bit, they did nothing to improve her mood. She stared out over the platform and for a moment felt acutely relieved. No one was there. No one on the platform. No one in the deserted station. No one anywhere. Maybe the Valkyrie had chickened out at the last minute. *Hope. Oh, hope.*

Probably Anna McGraw had thought twice about leaving home to travel with what she must think of as a bunch of loose women, playing in USO club dances, maybe going overseas and god only knew what else. Gillian's eyes swept the platform again, clinging to her flimsy little fantasy. Still no one.

Gillian turned to go. But as her eyes swept past the station doors she saw a figure loping toward her from the other side of the waiting room. Panting, the woman pushed open the door. She wasn't big boobed at all, or even blond. She was fine boned and wore her sable hair in a page boy. "I'm sorry," she began as she approached Gillian. "I'm afraid I'd fallen asleep and —"

With all her might, Gillian wished to sound blustery, impatient, and indignant. But the waiflike face, the sleepy, disheveled appearance, even the wide grin on Anna McGraw's face, stopped her. "Well, in this business, Miss McGraw," she squeaked, "— oh, forget it. I was sound asleep, too. C'mon. Let's climb aboard and get some shut-eye."

Anna followed Gillian to the coach and boarded. Gillian talked over her shoulder as they made their way down the darkened aisle. "We're at the Carlton. You'll room with Betse. You can't miss her. She plays the trombone and is shaped like one. Rehearsal at nine A.M. Sharp! And believe me, we'll need every second of it."

She's too slim, Gillian thought as she sagged into her seat. And too dainty. She'll never make it. With that happy thought, Gillian drifted into a fitful sleep as the train sped for Chicago.

On the following morning Gillian awoke rather late. The long train ride and lack of sleep had left her in a mood that hardly matched the cheeriness of the small hotel room she had checked into around four A.M. Relentless pink and yellow poured at her from every direction. There were floral drapes, opened at the window, yellow walls, and a vase of yellow flowers on a small writing table in the corner.

Sunshine streamed into the room through the rose-colored curtains. "Blast," she groaned and plunged her fingers deep into her mop of tangled hair.

The room, really only a cubicle, was in total disarray. Her instrument case, sheets of music, and her luggage cluttered the space. Gillian navigated carefully through the jumble and consulted her watch. Rehearsal in a half hour. There wasn't even time to shower. She put on a pair of slacks, a clean blouse and, to conceal her unruly hair, a knotted scarf. Blearily she made her way to the coffee shop in search of a steaming cup of java.

The coffee shop was busy. Its jangle, along with the smells of frying bacon, assaulted Gillian. Breakfast was her least favorite meal. She much preferred a cup of coffee and a couple of cigarettes. Several other Musi-Gals were in the coffee shop, although most seemed to be finished with breakfast and in the process of leaving. Gillian took a long pull on a Lucky Strike, a scalding swallow of coffee, and began to hatch a plan.

There would be absolutely no need, she decided, to allow Miss Fancy Pants, this Anna McGraw person, to do anything more than warm a chair during the rehearsal or, for that matter, the entire gig. There were plenty of instrumental numbers. And if what Phelps had hinted at over the last few months were true, then the band might get leave soon. After that, he also hinted, they might be shipped to the Pacific. Surely, somewhere in all of this she could replace Miss Opera. At that Gillian was able to experience the first happy moment she'd had since learning of Phelps's treachery and the appearance of little Miss Goody Two-shoes.

Gillian swept into the rehearsal hall at one minute after nine, juggling her saxophone and mounds of sheet music. She looked up on the stage and was pleased, as always, to see the band's setup. Each musician's stand was fronted with curved mother-of-pearl in pink with Musi-Gals written in script in red letters. The drums carried out the same motif. Most of the girls were already seated and had begun to warm up. Gillian strode to the stage. "Okay, everybody. Let's get going."

The cacophony of tuning dwindled away. "One O'Clock Jump," Gillian announced, and the musicians rustled through their folders. Gillian caught sight of Anna standing to the left of the stage. She looked at Gillian and smiled, a big genuine smile that showed rows of glistening white teeth. Gillian stared at her and again couldn't help but smile back. This morning, Anna McGraw looked much different from the way she had looked last night on the train platform. For one thing, there was a vivacity about her that she hadn't noticed, but of course they had both been much too sleepy on their first meeting. Gillian noted too the expensive but tailored clothes Anna wore and that her general demeanor, bearing, and looks all screamed polo-and-watercress-sandwich set as loud as a tympani roll in the 1812 Overture. "Be that as it may," Gillian uttered under her breath, "Anna McGraw occupies the only spot she'll fill on this gig. The sidelines." She raised her baton. "Now remember, Betse. That's B-flat at the coda. And-a-one, and-a-two."

Six

It was nearly one in the morning. Betse, Lil, Missy, and Gillian rode wearily in the back of a taxi. They were packed so tightly into the seat there was scarcely room to breathe. Four-way splits on cab fare saved a lot of money. Not that the Musi-Gals weren't paid well, for they were, given there was a war on. But it was always nice to have a little something extra for an occasional big splurge in one of the various cities they played.

The cab whooshed through lighted streets still surprisingly lively for the time of night. A light rain fell. Nobody seemed interested in talking. The rhythmic twack of the windshield wipers made the only sound. They were still in their stage clothes, low-cut gowns in various shades of pastel, and the backseat was a billow of tulle and net. Missy accidentally jammed the heel of her pump into Lil's ankle and murmured an apology. In the darkened silence someone else grumbled, "God, I hate these stinking dresses. Makes me feel like Little Bo Peep." Only a few dispirited grunts greeted the remark.

Gillian shifted uncomfortably and stared out the window at the throngs of soldiers and sailors weaving through the maze of neon. She twiddled with her necklace of fake pearls and tried to think of something pleasant. But Gillian had the sinking feeling she knew what was wrong. Usually after a gig, the girls laughed and chattered, letting off pent-up steam from the performance. But tonight felt as gloomy as winter rain. Once or twice she considered saying something but decided better of it; whatever was wrong wasn't something she particularly wanted to talk about. Not tonight anyway.

The cab finally dropped them off at the Carlton. The rumpled quartet rode an elevator to the mezzanine and from there took a small back staircase to rooms set aside for performers. Each said a desultory good-bye at her door. Gillian closed her own door behind her and immediately shed the hated pink gown. She hung the dress on a hanger, though she would have much preferred to stuff the thing into the waste can. The shoes she threw across the room in the general direction of the closet.

Clad only in her underwear she walked to the mirror and stared. Her face was heavily made up from the performance, and she wiped it carefully with tissue and cold cream. At the same time, she looked at herself with what she hoped was an uncritical eye. Here she was a grown woman, though she'd never divulge just how grown, and still a liberal salting of freckles dotted her cheeks and nose. She pulled her dark red hair back from her brow to apply cold cream. She wasn't a beauty, at least by current standards, but she was nonetheless pleased with her appearance.

She continued to apply cold cream in wide swaths and methodically remove it with wads of tissue. Her skin showed the stress of the last few months — shadows, fatigue, and even the appearance of crow's feet. She wiped a slather of cream from her lips, removing every trace of the harsh red lipstick.

"Okay. So I ain't Ina Rae Hutton." she said to her reflection. "But at least I'm not driving rivets or typing insurance letters."

For a moment Gillian allowed herself the luxury of a forbidden thought. In a way she was glad the war had happened. A blasphemous, probably even treasonous, thought these days. She deplored killing and death and the very notion that violence was the accepted method of dealing with conflict. Powerless to stop any of it, however, she enjoyed an avenue of escape and a freedom she could have but dreamt of before the war.

She had been born rather late in life to a pair of aging vaudevillians, and her life had always been filled with music and talk of the stage. Her mother was nearing forty when Gillian was born and her father well past fifty. Her birth coincided with the virtual twilight of vaudeville, and Gillian had always suspected she had been planned as a substitute for the intense joys of life in front of the footlights.

Her father came from England in 1916 to work with an American troupe and had promptly met and married Gillian's mother, Elaine, who at the time aspired to the classical stage. Together they worked out a song-and-dance routine and spent several years happily entertaining the slowly diminishing audiences in gaudy vaudeville halls around the country. At length the audiences dwindled to almost nil and, sensing the end of an era, the Pettibones repaired to Mrs. Pettibone's family home, a moderately decrepit three-story Victorian just outside Poughkeepsie. Several of their friends followed, doubtless drawn to the company and the number of commodious rooms. Without any real planning or effort, their home became a boarding house catering to ex-vaudevillians, out-of-work musicians, and those for whom fame had proven elusive.

Gillian was born quite late one night in an upstairs bedroom while downstairs a jam session was in progress. The very first sounds she heard were her mother's delighted squeals and the syncopated strains of "Maple Leaf Rag."

In time Gillian's father died, the number of boarders dwindled, and Hitler invaded Poland. Gillian's mother began to talk about selling the house and moving to California. She had a sister there and imagined life for herself and Gillian would be better there than in Poughkeepsie.

Gillian thought otherwise. She didn't mind leaving

Poughkeepsie, but not to live with her mother and her aunt in a tiny bungalow in San Diego and probably land a job as an assembly line riveter in a defense plant. Besides, her mother and aunt constantly pestered her about her lack of male friends. Fearing she would become an old maid, they took upon themselves the task of turning their charge into proper marriage bait. "Bah," she said when the clucking and fussing became more than she could bear. "I have music. What do I need with men?"

She toyed with the idea of forming a band, but didn't really know whether anyone would hire them or even want to listen. By chance one afternoon Gillian ran into an ex-boarder, a thin young man with a lopsided smile. They went to the local cafe for coffee, and there Gillian learned that the young man and another fellow had gotten up a juggling act and were getting all the gigs they could handle by playing for the USO. Gillian went home and gave this information a thorough going over for the next week. The week following that she made phone calls and wrote letters. Two months later she arrived at the USO office with three other musicians in tow, all of them excellent players and all of them female. They auditioned, and the USO, pronouncing them a novelty act, signed the Musi-Gals for a tour of duty.

Seven

The Musi-Gals had played their third night of the Chicago gig, and again a taxi deposited them at the front door of the hotel. As before, no one spoke. Laughter and good-humored joshing seemed a dimly remembered thing of the past. They piled out of the cab and went directly and silently to their respective rooms.

Gillian fell immediately into bed in a wallow of confusion and weariness. Nolan Phelps's face swam before her. She could see his pinched little smirk and his watery eyes. She couldn't shake the apparition, and instead of falling asleep she began to recount the many times Phelps had tried to sabotage her and the band. Anna McGraw was hardly the first.

One time in Seattle they had been given the wrong booking date. When the band arrived for a four-night stand, they were shocked to find another orchestra already playing. Phelps claimed the incident was merely a paperwork snafu, but Gillian suspected that Phelps was the only snafu.

The more Gillian tossed, the more her mind barged back through her trials with Phelps, and the more she knew she'd get little sleep. Sleep came with the dawn and only after Gillian's firm commitment — to herself, to the Musi-Gals, and to god in heaven, for good measure. "He won't get away with it this time."

Gillian awoke slowly and reluctantly, tangled in her sheets and blanket. Someone was banging on her door. "Jeez, it must be the middle of the night," she mumbled. "Who the hell —" She untangled herself and went to the door. "Who is it?" she croaked.

"Me, Lil," came a voice on the other side of the door. "Open up, Pettibone. I've got some coffee for you."

Gillian opened the door. In contrast to her own rumpled appearance, Lil looked bright and snappy. Lil handed the coffee through the door. "Here. Get some of this in you." Gillian took a gulp, and Lil followed her into the tiny room.

"Sorry," Lil said, although she didn't seem in the least so. "We've been waiting for you to come downstairs. When you didn't, we thought maybe we should just come up and get you."

"We? We who?" Gillian took another sip of coffee.

"Just have a little more coffee, then we'll talk, okay? Boy, you're a sleepyhead today."

"Wha' time is it?" Gillian asked.

"Nearly noon."

"Whoa." Gillian flopped down on the side of the bed, clutching the cup of coffee. "I couldn't sleep," she muttered. "I didn't miss rehearsal, did I?"

"No. No rehearsal this morning, remember?" Lil pulled up a chair and sat down. "Listen, we've got to talk."

Gillian managed a smile, then a question. "So, what's up? What's so all-fired important?"

Lil looked directly into Gillian's face. Without a trace of humor she announced, "We're laying an egg, Pettibone."

The coffee cup shook in her hand; coffee splashed onto Gillian's nightshirt. There. It had been said. The cat was out of the bag.

Lil waited only long enough for Gillian to wipe up the spilled coffee. "There's more," she said. "Seems like the manager of the club has already called Phelps. He's flipping mad. Says he was promised low-cut gowns and tits. Says all he got was a bunch of dames sitting around playing instruments."

"What did Phelps say?" Gillian asked in a whisper, the coffee cup again shaking precariously.

"Don't know. All I know is the manager wants to see you downstairs. On the double."

"You know what the problem is as well as I do, Lil. We don't have a lead singer."

"Yeah, I know, kiddo. But we've got to get one.

This guy wants big white teeth and plenty of tits standing at the microphone singing love songs."

"I just don't know what to do," Gillian almost wailed. "I know the audience hasn't been all that receptive."

"Receptive? They're asleep by the third number."

"But Lil, all we've got is an opera singer — one who never sang with a swing band. What am I supposed to do?"

"I know it's a problem. And I know how you feel about it." Lil paused to light a cigarette. She blew a narrow cloud of smoke. It was one of her favorite gestures, that and pulling her Veronica Lake hairdo off her face to tuck behind her earlobe. "But listen, Gillian. You can't let your ongoing war with Phelps get in the way here. Just go on downstairs and talk to the USO guy. Try to work something out. Maybe I could fill in, uh, temporarily, that is."

"Right. When pigs fly," Gillian muttered under her breath while searching her closet for something to wear. Lil could play a mean bass fiddle, but sing? The woman would need an armload of bags to carry the simplest tune.

A few minutes later, Gillian entered the coffee shop and saw the USO manager sitting at a booth along the far wall. She joined him at his table and noticed he was halfway through the blueplate special. She ordered coffee. "Lil says you wanted to see me," she said after the waitress left.

"Yeah," he said through a mouthful of corned beef hash. "Got to spice up your act."

"I thought we'd been playing pretty well," Gillian said.

"Umph," he said, "true enough. In fact, you play as well as the best of them. But that ain't what I mean." He took another bite and chewed it thoughtfully. "See, it's like this. We got guys in here from all over. We got dance hostesses; we got refreshments; we got smuggled-in booze. What we don't got is a couple of canaries in low-cut dresses singing love songs." He paused to stare at Gillian. "And that we gotta have."

"One of our singers canceled out at the last minute," Gillian offered. "We haven't had time to — ah — to replace her." Gillian knew she was fumbling, but she plunged ahead. "We're doing everything we can, believe me."

"Okay, I'll believe you," the manager interrupted. "Just be sure you've done it by tomorrow night's performance. Phelps wants a call from me by then. If it ain't fixed, it's your funeral."

Gillian sat staring at her now cold coffee long after the manager had finished his meal and left. She was in her least favorite place — the corner. She looked toward the front of the room where several band members were seated at the counter. "Damn," she muttered under her breath. "Damn it all."

They all looked anxiously at her as she approached the luncheon counter. "So, what happened?" Betse asked.

"Let's just say we're going to put Anna McGraw through finishing school. Betse, get your roomie to the rehearsal hall in twenty minutes. Somebody tell Sue Ellen to bring her piano scores. I'll bring the vocals and meet you all there."

"Well, okay," Betse piped. "But you sure as hell don't look happy about it."

"That, m'dear, has got to be the understatement of the year. Anyway, who says anyone has a right to be happy?"

"Hey, c'mon. Maybe it won't be as bad as all that. She can at least read music. Plus, we've got rhythm aplenty among the seven of us. Maybe it'll rub off." Betse tried to sound hopeful

"Yeah, and if that doesn't work, we'll cram it down her throat until her girdle pops." With this Gillian swept out of the coffee shop. She needed time to compose herself.

Later she walked along the carpeted, stale-smelling hallway leading to the rehearsal. "Just face it, Pettibone," she said to herself. "Go in there and get it over with. If we have to stay till midnight tonight and every night till kingdom come, we'll make a swing singer out of our little diva." She continued down the hall, rounded a corner, and pushed on the door of the rehearsal hall.

Gillian froze, her hand jammed against the partially open door. Anna McGraw stood at the mike. Sue Ellen played piano, a huge grin lighting her face. Betse's trombone sounded like satin, its bell pointing skyward. Missy played a short rill, ending with a cymbal crash. Every member of the band was there except Lil. Gillian shook her head vigorously but continued staring at Anna McGraw, her mouth slightly ajar. Anna wore pleated pants and a white blouse with a light sweater knotted around her shoulders. She was barefoot, though this was a fact Gillian hardly noticed. What she did notice, and notice with quickening pulse, was that Anna McGraw could sing the roof down.

Snapping fingers and smiles of approval greeted

Gillian as she inched her way closer to the stage. Not only could the little diva sing, she knew what to do with her body. Her hands gripped the microphone, her feet wide apart and her head thrown back. Her face was flushed with music. The song poured out, and Anna McGraw's singing could make a person believe she really did have "the sun in the morning and the moon at night," and what's more, be glad for her. It was no less than her due.

Gillian stared. Anna sang. Soon, Gillian's feet began tapping, her alto voice joined Anna's. By the second chorus, a wide smile replaced her open-mouthed surprise. Anna caught Gillian's eye, and it wasn't exactly triumph Gillian saw there but a certain blaze of good-natured redemption.

"I really don't blame you," Anna said later, after the rest of the band had gone for a break. "You were put in a heck of a spot. I know you must have been really rattled about the opera thing." Anna paused and looked into the middle distance. Then, with a little grin, she said, "I was rattled, too."

"Well, sure, ah sure. I guess so." Gillian grinned back. Why had her tongue departed her? "I never thought about it that way. But I guess you must have been wary of us, too."

"Oh, sure thing. I never meant to upset the apple cart around here, and I knew you must be upset about my past singing experience. I had hoped to grab a minute of your time, ah, privately, and talk about my singing. But I guess Lil had other ideas. It was sort of a command performance I just gave."

"What do you mean?"

"Well, it was Lil that suggested I sing a number or two during break. She thought it might be the only chance I got to sing with you guys." Anna looked up at Gillian with a sideways grin, cleared her throat, and went on. "In fact, she was adamant, wouldn't take no for an answer. She even made the rest of the band stay for the session. But you weren't there, and I didn't want to audition without you. I'm glad you came in when you did."

Anna winked, and for a reason well beyond Gillian's ken, she blushed. "I'm glad, too. You're great. But I'm confused. How come your bio says you're an operatic singer?"

"Singing opera was my mother's idea really. She loved that kind of music, wanted to study classical voice herself. But then she met my father, and the rest is history."

"So he didn't like opera?"

"He was very rich and good looking. He didn't need to like opera to snag my mother."

"Does this mean you don't get along with your folks?"

"Oh, no. They're okay. I just don't want to be like them, that's all. There's more to life than posh parties and dashing off to the Continent two or three times a year. Of course, the war put a stop to that part, but the party goes on just like always."

Anna sat down behind the drums and, giving the bass drum a couple of taps, played herself a drum roll intro. "Anyhow, when I volunteered at the USO they asked about singing lessons and where I had sung. Of course, all I could truthfully say was opera. That was months ago. I thought I'd never hear from them again."

"Hmmm," Gillian said. "So you sing opera but don't want to, and you can belt out the pop music like a pro. And you probably don't need money, so you're here to help with the cause."

"Yep. That and to have a little fun."

"By the way, how did you learn to sing like that?"

Anna winked again at Gillian and smiled. "It's in my bones. I've been singing this kind of music for years. But only to the radio, and only in my room."

The Musi-Gals came through the door. Usually they straggled back from a break and inevitably someone had to go fish somebody out of the john or the coffee shop. Gillian smiled and nodded, giving each the **V** for victory sign as they trooped into the hall. "Hey, where's Lil?" she asked after a moment.

"She fell off the roof," someone answered.

"Yeah, bad timing too. She only heard the first few bars of our new canary warble a tune," Betse added. "What a time to get her period, huh?"

Everyone took their places and waited for Gillian to announce the next number. "Chattanooga Choo Choo," she called. "Everybody got it? McGraw, you got sheet music?"

"Yes, I've got it," Anna answered. "Ready when you are, professor."

The reeds started the buildup, then Betse came in on trombone. Anna stood shoulder to shoulder with Gillian, and on exactly the right cue they began the song. When it was over they beamed and hugged each other while the Musi-Gals applauded. Amid the whistling and clapping someone called out, "She's the berries! She's better than Della. You guys are the tops! What a pair!"

Gillian and Anna took it all in — Gillian bursting with enthusiasm and Anna looking as if she was about to cry. When the ruckus died down Gillian called for two more vocal numbers, and the band set happily to work. When the rehearsal was over, Betse hugged Gillian and said, "Your voices sound perfect together. You two are a real match." Betse grabbed her arm as she started for the door. "Looks like it's not Anna McGraw's girdle that's popping. It's this band."

"Looks like it all right," Gillian said, grinning. "I was so wrong about this. Forgive me?"

"Sure, sweetheart. Just don't get pigheaded on us again." Betse gave Gillian a big smile. Gillian turned and fairly floated to her room for a rest before the night's show.

Instead of rest she got a knock on her door. She opened it and there stood Anna, dressed just as before but this time wearing shoes, loafers with a penny in each. "Come in," Gillian said. "Take a load off. By the way, if you don't mind my asking, why were you barefoot today? It's no big thing really, I'm just curious."

"Oh, just one of my little quirks," Anna responded. "I like to sing barefoot. It's only my imagination I'm sure, but I just feel the music better with my shoes off."

"Well, whatever it takes," Gillian grinned. "You sure made a hit today."

"Let's hope I do tonight as well." Anna walked over and stood by the window. "I thought of something else I want to say to you." Anna turned to face Gillian. "I've already heard all the stories about you and Phelps. It must really get your goat to have him pull one over on you."

"Well, yes. But this time it backfired on him. You really can sing. Phelps is the one with egg on his face."

"What a germ. He didn't give a care whether I made a fool of myself or not. He was just out to get you. Ugh, men!"

"Right! But Phelps came up stinking on this one. This time I got the upper hand. Or rather, we did."

"You're very brave," Anna said. "I admire that. You're ready to fly in the face of the almighty, I imagine, when you feel you're right."

"I suppose." Gillian's color rose a little. She didn't get many compliments about such virtues as bravery and spunk. "I truly do try to put the band first. It's just harder if I'm fighting my personal battles as well."

"Hey, don't I know it," Anna exclaimed as though a seasoned veteran of such battles herself. "And one more thing. Don't you just hate it when those jerks like Phelps and the club manager get so engrossed over bare bosoms they can't even see the talent behind 'em. You guys are really good. Someday you should try to make a record or something. I suppose I should say *we* guys now."

"Yeah, it's a real pain in the rump, the way they act. Makes you feel discounted, as if playing a musical instrument and playing it well is only the second most important thing." Gillian scowled and grabbed the hem of her pastel gown still hanging in its protective sleeve from the cleaners. "Just to prove my point, look at these dresses. There's practically no fabric from the waist up. Sometimes I'm afraid my boobs will fall out."

Anna guffawed. "And then everywhere else there's so much material you have to turn sideways to get through a doorway."

"Exactly, except at the waist. They're so tight there, with all the staves pinching your skin and all, that it's often hard to get a deep enough breath to sustain a long solo." Gillian knew she was smiling, even though the topic at hand was a big bone of contention between herself and Phelps.

"Ever thought about changing the costume to something a little less restrictive?" Anna asked, casting a critical eye on the mountain of pink net.

"Well, once. But I'm not sure it turned out to be all that much of an improvement. At least we're not running around in swimsuits with bright pink bows pinned to our rumps."

Anna grinned, and for the first time Gillian saw a delightful flash of mischievousness, and not a small amount of good-natured rebellion.

"Maybe we should try again," Anna said and let the hem of the pink formal flutter to the carpeted floor.

"You know. Maybe we should do just that." Gillian winked.

Eight

The Musi-Gals scored big in Chicago and were held over an extra week in Jersey. Ditto Philly. Now they were on the road, anticipating a triumphant entry into Milwaukee aboard a chartered Trailways bus. Everywhere they played, soldiers and sailors jammed the halls to see, hear, and applaud them.

A few miles back they had begun singing "Ninety-Nine Bottles of Beer on the Wall," and after ten or so renditions all the way through, some were getting hoarse but no one was in the mood to stop. Having exhausted their ample supply of bawdy numbers, the band had been forced to begin a chorus of rounds.

Gillian and Anna sat together in the two seats just behind the driver, singing as loud as anyone. They had, however, sat out several rounds so they could stay in voice for the evening performance. The bus rounded a sharp curve and as it did so, Anna jumped to her feet at the front of the aisle, steadying herself with the handrail. "Wait!" she exclaimed. She waved her arms wildly in the air. "Hey, listen up, I've remembered another one. It's to the tune of 'Sweet Betsy from Pike.' It goes like this." Anna belted out the lyrics, noticing the bus driver's neck and ears were soon bright red.

After the song was over, Anna plopped down again next to Gillian. "Boy, that one was really raunchy," Gillian said.

"I know. I learned it from another student of Madame Scala, my voice instructor." Anna playfully jostled Gillian's shoulder.

"We've been hanging around together almost constantly for weeks," Gillian said with a wide grin, "and you never cease to amaze me."

"Nor you me." Anna gave Gillian a sweet, almost embarrassed, smile.

They settled back into their seats, arms touching. Gillian feeling inordinately happy. She entertained the possibility that Anna might be wearing some exotic talc, for it seemed the tiny hairs on their arms shared in a most exquisite electricity.

At the hotel, everyone tumbled off the bus. In a

short time they gathered in the hotel's ballroom, a cavernous room, high and long. From the tall ceiling hung a huge, mirrored globe. Someone had neglected to switch off the globe, and so it turned slowly, sending little bursts of light dancing across the floors, walls, and ceiling.

There was a warm, damp feeling about the fine old ballroom, made the more swampy by the hotel's ancient water-cooled air conditioning. The smell was of damp straw and stale smoke. Gillian took a deep breath of it and eyed the deserted ballroom. This was her kind of place. The smell of it, the sound of musicians tuning, even the faint smell of last night's passion, the sweat of raptured dancers. For a giddy moment, she wanted to run and find Anna and drag her in here. For what? To experience it with her. To smell the dancers. To dance.

Shaking her head, Gillian strode through the double doorway, her shirt clinging to her moist back. She hardly noticed the cloying dampness, her head too full of confusion and craziness and wanting to dance with Anna. There was hardly time to dwell on the images bouncing around in her head. The ballroom was alive with excitement and activity; there was a very big surprise in store for the night's audience, especially for Nolan Phelps.

No one sat still, and no one could keep quiet. Bustling and chattering were everywhere. And in all of that heady atmosphere, Gillian could distinguish, without meaning to, the distinct presence of Anna McGraw. They had drawn so close in so short a time.

That fact was a delicious icing on the cake as far as Gillian was concerned. She had a wonderful new friend, a band on the rise, and tonight they would unveil an entirely new image for the soon to be famous Musi-Gals. Gillian, though both her clothing and her hair felt soggy, moved excitedly through the spangled ballroom.

"Missy, hi." She waggled her fingers high in the air. "Are the trunks unloaded yet?"

Missy chewed her stick of Juicy Fruit all the harder and nodded in the affirmative.

"You know, kiddo," Gillian sang out as she glided past, "Next week we'll add 'Accentuate the Positive' to the vocal numbers. How about it?"

Missy grinned and blew a huge bubble that broke and splattered.

Gillian mounted the bandstand and began distributing sheet music with the aura of one just gone from frog to prince. They had gigs lined up from as far as the eye could see, and there was no way Phelps could deny them the promised trip to the Pacific theater, not if he knew what was good for him. And into the bargain had been tossed the least expected but most wondrous turn of all, Anna McGraw, co-conspirator and best friend. Gillian, for the very first time in her life, wanted to learn more about opera.

The band took their places for a short rehearsal. The performance would begin at eight o'clock sharp, and they had already heard that the Philly *Inquirer,* the USO, and even the *Stars and Stripes* reviewers would be in attendance — not an occasion to mess with. After a run-through of all the tunes, the band members drifted off to their rooms or to the lobby for a few quiet hours before they had to reassemble backstage.

Gillian wandered around the potted ferns and red leather furniture of the lobby for a while, occasionally dragging on a Lucky Strike, far too excited to think of a nap. In the lobby bar she allowed herself one Rob Roy, and as the liquid slid down her throat she found herself pondering her fateful meeting with Anna McGraw. She took another pull from her fresh Lucky and smiled, shaking her head. One never knows when fate is primed and ready to pounce. A few months ago she wouldn't have dreamed of someone coming along who would take the Musi-Gals as seriously as did she — yet alone someone as witty, fun to be around, and devilish as Anna. The gods were smiling, Gillian knew, for she could not remember so blessed a time. Gillian realized that she thought of Anna almost all the time, just as she was doing now. What the heck. Anna was fun and smart. Why shouldn't she think often of such a person?

In her own room, Anna wasn't having any luck counting sheep, so she got up from her still made bed, washed her face, and descended the grand staircase to the plant littered lobby bar. At once she saw Gillian, sitting between a hanging fern and a poster of Uncle Sam with a warning finger to his lips.

"Hi," she said and eased herself onto the

leatherette stool next to her friend. A sailor sitting on Gillian's left ran a comb through his hair in preparation for a little small talk, but noticed, perceptively, that as soon as Anna was seated the world around the two nice looking ladies seemed to draw closed around them. He turned his attention back to his warming beer.

"What are you having?" Anna asked.

"A Rob Roy."

"Fine. I'll have the same." Anna smiled at the bartender.

"So, Pettibone," she toasted as her drink arrived, "here's to the new, improved Musi-Gals. You're a damn musical genius."

"Hardly," Gillian said, but raised her glass anyway. She grinned and clinked her glass against Anna's. "What brings you here at this hour?"

"Oh, just couldn't relax, I guess. Too excited." Anna looked at Gillian over the top of her glass and smiled.

Suddenly and inexplicably, Gillian could think of nothing to say. She turned around, staring into the mirror behind the bar. A radio played some Tex Beneke tune, but not so loudly as to compete with the noise in Gillian's brain. Endless possible conversations, all of them witty, meaningful, wondrous, and filled with insight eluded her. "I'm glad you showed up," she finally managed. "I was feeling far too excited for a nap myself." Anna smiled and looked at her companion for a long moment.

The color in Gillian's cheeks rose as she stared at the place on the bar stool where her espadrilles tapped restlessly on the shiny chrome. "It's a big night tonight. And, I guess, well, I just couldn't relax. Actually, I wanted someone to share the anticipation with. And presto, here you are."

Anna smiled and nodded, placing her hand on Gillian's shoulder. "Just wait till they get a load of our new look. And, of course, our swinging sound." Anna squeezed Gillian then returned her arm, somewhat slowly, to her lap.

"You betcha. And it's all due to you, McGraw." Gillian lifted her highball and wiggled it in the air. She suddenly felt very lightheaded.

"Not so," replied Anna. "You just needed an accomplice, that's all."

"Yes, an accomplice," Gillian laughed. "Great choice of terms."

"Then, let's have a toast. To accomplices everywhere." Anna raised her glass and clinked it against the side of Gillian's.

"Here, here," said Gillian, still grinning. "Did you know that the dictionary defines an accomplice as 'one associated with another, especially in wrongdoing.' "

"Most interesting," Anna replied with a raised eyebrow. "Personally, I'm game for a little wrongdoing, especially if the doing is directed at the more notable wrongdoers of this world. Among them, of course, our own Mr. Phelps." Anna tilted her chin upward, ran a hand through her hair, and winked. "So then. Here's to a long and happy accomplicement. To us."

"To us," Gillian toasted, aware of a lump in her

throat at the very mention of the two of them as a pair.

"To Pettibone and McGraw," Anna toasted and finished hers.

"Want another?" the bartender asked, swooping to his customers.

"No, thanks, none for me," Gillian mimed a dizzy spell, which wasn't all that difficult.

"Me either." Anna paid for her drink. "The Misses Pettibone and McGraw will be taking their leave." She turned to go, grabbing Gillian's arm. "Never mix booze and pleasure, young man." Anna shook her finger playfully. "Or is that booze and business."

Crossing the lobby Gillian suddenly stopped and said, "You know, Anna, I'm tired of calling you McGraw. It's so, so impersonal, or something."

"I know what you mean, Pettibone, but it seems that using just last names is all the rage these days."

"I'm sure it has a lot to do with all the freedom we're feeling. No Missus, no Miss, no first names even, like the guys have been doing forever. In a way I really like it, but I feel like I want to call you Anna. It's such a pretty name."

"Then, by all means, call me Anna. And what shall I call you?"

"You could call me Gilly. My dad used to call me that when I was little, and I like it."

"Gilly it is." They linked arms and at the top of the staircase took separate hallways to their respective rooms.

* * * * *

By seven-thirty a crowd had gathered in the ballroom. Gillian heard people milling around, laughing, talking, and clinking silver and glass. As yet, however, she couldn't see the crowd because tonight, for the first time ever, the show would begin with a darkened house, soft lights, and a slowly rising curtain. Usually they just paraded out onto a stage, bare except for their music stands and instruments. Everything had been changed to the special lighting, the raising of the heavy burgundy curtain, and last, but certainly not least, the new performance outfits.

Backstage was a frenzy. Marge frantically sewed snaps on her cummerbund while Lil and Betse glued glitter to several top hats. Missy wound the ends of her drum sticks with red, white, and blue ribbons. Anna perched atop a stool, looking resplendent in her stage clothes. Someone hurried by and asked her to sew a button on her coat, which she did, biting off the extra string with her teeth. At that moment Gillian walked in, and Anna had to grab the stool she sat on to keep from flying across the floor to hug her. She looked magnificent. Everybody looked great, but Gillian had that something extra — perhaps her height or her unruly red hair. Anna couldn't be sure just what. Gillian had the elan and style to go with the outfit and even complement it.

Gillian started across the floor toward Anna, but Lil intercepted and took Gillian aside. "Say, Pettibone. Are you sure we're not making a mistake here?"

"Huh?" Gillian looked amazed.

Lil tucked a tress of her Veronica Lake hair

behind her ear. "Well, just look at all of this, and at us. We look like a bunch of guys. Or dykes."

"You're not serious!" Gillian yelped. "How can you say such a thing?" Her gut started a low roll.

"Top hats, cummerbunds, bow ties. What next, Pettibone? Fatigues?"

"I don't know what you mean, Lil. Why the hell didn't you speak up sooner, if you're all that upset." Gillian sucked her breath in and struggled to reply. *Dykes?* Maybe there were a few women like that in the world, but they wore? — they did? — Oh, who the hell knew what they wore, never mind *did*. What had gotten into Lil anyway?

"I don't know. Everybody else seemed so excited about the new outfits. I just didn't say anything. Now that it's all been done and I've tried on this monkey suit, well, I just don't like it. I don't look good in tights."

"You look fine," Gillian said, still puzzled. "What's gotten into you anyway?"

"Nothing has gotten into me, I'm just worried, that's all. What if we bomb? What if Phelps finds out and causes a big stink? He's not going to like this one bit."

"I wasn't aware you and Phelps had any love lost between you. What's going on, Lil? Are you really worried about the band, or just the way you think you look in tights?"

"The band," Lil said and lit up a Lucky. She blew a stream of smoke.

"But I don't get it. Things are going great. We're a hit. Since when are you so all-fired concerned?"

"Since the Musi-Gals started becoming the Gillian and Anna show." Lil blew out another long stream of smoke. Lil turned on her heel and stomped away, leaving Gillian to stare at her departing back with a mixture of anger and bewilderment. Dykes! Gillian thought she might have seen one once. Someone's friend at the boarding house. But that woman weighed over two hundred pounds. She had Brill Cream-styled men's hair that bore the marks of a comb, wore a man's suit, and even sported a pair of men's wing tips. Lil must be out of her mind. Nothing about Anna McGraw, or herself for that matter, bore the slightest resemblance.

At a few minutes past eight, the burgundy curtain opened and revealed a stage set with red, white, and blue. A huge flag covered the area behind the band, and even the pink mother-of-pearl music stands had been hung with red, white, and blue bunting. Three big spotlights at the back of the ballroom swept the stage. Into all of this light and color paraded the Musi-Gals, to thunderous applause.

They wore dark blue tights, red tuxedo jackets, and shirtwaists made of silver spangles. Each wore a top hat, also decked out in spangles. The clip-on bow ties were red, white, and blue stripes, as were the cummerbunds. The last two performers to take the stage were Gillian and Anna, who loped into the spotlight holding hands.

Nine

A heavy fog had rolled in from the Pacific during the night. The planes on the runway sat like huddled ghosts in the dim morning. Lil sat huddled on a trunk on the tarmac outside the Army airfield in San Diego. She chain-smoked and stared at the hint of sun barely showing through the thick bank of mist and fog. Her face looked set in stone, and she endlessly fiddled with her hair.

Inside the ready room, which struck Gillian as anything but, mailbags, boxes, and service personnel vied for the available space. Most of the girls lounged on the army-issue benches. Betse leafed through a two-month-old copy of *The Saturday Evening Post* while chewing feverishly on her hard-to-come-by contraband Double Bubble gum — Betse had a friend in the Quartermaster Corps. Sue Ellen wrote a letter to her beau, already in action in the Pacific.

Gillian slouched in a chair, her legs straight out in front, hands folded over her midsection. Anna tried to coax a bottle of Coke out of a vending machine by giving the machine a solid kick. She purchased a bag of peanuts, poured them into the top of her Coca-Cola, and wandered over to plop heavily beside Gillian.

"Boy, am I beat. What time is it and how long have we been waiting now?"

"It's eleven, so that means we've been stranded here for over six hours." Gillian remained in her position in the chair, legs out, eyes closed. "But they tell me the fog is beginning to lift and we can get going pretty soon." Having said that, Gillian opened her eyes and looked at Anna. "You antsy, too?"

"Uh uh," Anna shrugged. "Just filled with anticipation. I hate to say it, but I feel as if I'm going on a long exotic vacation. I can hardly wait to get out of here." With that Anna assumed the same position Gillian seemed to be so much enjoying. She slouched in the chair and slid her long legs out in front of her.

Anna looked at the pair of legs thrust halfway across the aisle and smiled. When Gillian noticed the smile and the reason for it, she grinned broadly. Their legs were encased in army-issue khaki twill, smartly seamed, their feet in sensible brown oxfords. They wore khaki shirts and army-issue slacks with button fronts and back pockets. Helmets were stowed somewhere in their gear. Sooner or later, the suitcases carrying their clothes would catch up with them. Thank god, the instruments were there.

"Neat, eh?" Gilly smiled.

"Sure thing, professor. And comfy too."

After their gig in Milwaukee where they had played to stomping, applauding, yelling audiences, the band had been given leave. Gilly left for San Diego and a visit to her mother. Anna departed for Saint Louis. While home, Gilly spent her time catching up on her sleep and gabbing with her mother, but mostly mooning around, missing Anna. She took long walks and spent lazy afternoons sitting on the front porch, chin in hand, watching workers file in and out of the defense plant across the way. Sometimes she tried to read. But mostly she thought about Anna.

Once Gilly's mother had even said something about her state, saying she must be in love. Why else would she act so goofy? Gilly turned away quickly, muttering about how tiring life with the band had become. Long before her leave was over, she began wishing she were back with the band — back with Anna.

They were together again, smoking Luckies and waiting for the fog to lift. When the skies cleared enough for takeoff they would be Manila bound, headed for the Pacific and the real war — and to

Camp Pershing at that, the main base of operations for USO entertainers. Word of the band's success had spread quickly around the bases and USO clubs stateside and had traveled overseas as well. Not even Nolan Phelps could stop their assignment to play for the troops in the Pacific theater. The Musi-Gals, with their perky, patriotic costumes, were just what the doctor ordered.

Gillian sensed people milling around her chair and opened one eye to gaze. Marge, Sue Ellen, and Betse were there. "Hey," they said in unison.

"Hey, yourself," Gillian said. "What's up? Are we leaving now?"

"Nope. Still waiting for the weather to clear." Betse knelt beside Gillian and said in a highly conspiratorial tone, "Just what the hell is the matter with Lil?"

Gilly sat upright and adjusted her pant legs. "Lil? What do you mean?" Though Gillian had heard the question she wanted to stall the answer. The business with Lil puzzled and angered her. Lil had been a true-blue trouper since the band was first formed. But since Anna had come aboard, she seemed to be drawing farther and farther away, from both Gillian and the Musi-Gals.

"I mean," Betse went on, "that I asked her if she wouldn't like to come inside and get a little warmer, not to mention drier. You know what she said?" Betse paused for a moment before launching into a Garbo imitation. "Leave me alone," Betse vamped. "I don't know, but it looks like she's ready to have a cow. Say, what's up?"

"I really don't know, Betse," Gillian said slowly. "Maybe she just doesn't like waiting in airports.

Maybe she's on the rag again and needs an aspirin. I don't think there's much to worry about. Just let her be. When we get to Camp Pershing I'll talk with her."

"Know what I think?" Betse volunteered. "I think she's jealous."

"Of what, for heaven's sake?"

"Well, for one thing, I think she really wanted to replace Della. And instead, you teamed up with a newcomer. I think she's doing a slow burn."

"But she can't sing!"

"I know that. You know that. The whole band knows that." Betse leaned down closer, "But Lil doesn't know that."

"Ohhh." Gilly rubbed her hand over her chin. "I didn't think she was serious about singing. She only talked to me about it once."

"Well, try to get in a word with her sometime soon, huh? Rumor has it that she's been on the phone to Phelps lately, maybe about the new uniforms — hell, I don't know what about. But talk to her, will ya?"

"Yeah. Sure thing. Soon as we're settled in at Pershing I'll have a little chat with Lil. Maybe we could have a bass fiddle solo on one of the jazzier numbers. I'll talk to her and try to straighten it out."

Betse and the others walked away to whatever slim entertainment might be found in the Quonset hut waiting area. Anna looked at Gillian. Her gaze was questioning. "What's really up with Lil? Do you know?"

Gillian chose not to mention the conversation she had with Lil backstage in Milwaukee. Lil's remarks, her suspicions, had left such a bad taste in Gilly's mouth, she opted to keep them to herself. "I don't know," she lied. Gilly reached into her shirt pocket and extracted a Baby Ruth. She tore the paper wrapping away and took a huge bite. There was no power on earth that could make her repeat the nasty words Lil had spoken. She munched the candy bar with a pretense of gastronomical delight.

"I have something I need to confide in you," Anna said, reaching over and snapping off a full third of Gillian's candy bar. "I don't think Lil likes me." Anna shoved the candy bar into her mouth and began chewing. "She never speaks to me, and when she does I almost wish she hadn't."

Gillian studied Anna's face. "Why do you think she doesn't like you? I can't think of a single reason why anybody would dislike you." She winked at Anna and kept chewing.

Anna flushed and looked down, her eyes dewy. Hands in her lap she went on. "That was really sweet, Pettibone." After a moment Anna looked up. "Back to the subject at hand, though. I think she's jealous. It's just a feeling. Nothing I could prove. And something else — she always looks at me like she's suspicious of something."

"It probably has nothing to do with you. Lil has never been known for her gregarious personality and winning smile. Forget it. She's just being Lil."

Anna seemed only slightly mollified, but she turned her attention back to her Coke and peanuts. Gillian, however, continued to pore over the growing rift with Lil. Why on earth would anyone, especially one of the band, want to turn on the group now? Everything was headed their way. Surely Lil would come to her senses soon enough. In a matter of hours they would begin playing shows all over the Pacific and Lil would hardly have time to launch a full-scale snit.

"Don't take it to heart," Gillian murmured into Anna's ear when she noticed the other woman staring pensively toward Lil. "She's just having a prolonged bad mood about something or other. I think Lil is the only person I know who possesses not a shred of a sense of humor."

Anna straightened in her seat and brushed candy crumbs from her shirt. "Hey, maybe she's just sitting out there on that trunk trying to melt the fog with the sheer heat of her mood. In which case, more power to her. I'm ready to be airborne."

Just then the staticky PA system came on, "Army troop carrier cleared for landing. All passengers for Camp Pershing assemble on the tarmac at gate 1B."

No one waited for the announcement to be repeated. Scampering feet and clamor and colliding instrument cases engulfed the tiny Quonset. If everything went well, the morning sun would find the Musi-Gals at the center of the Pacific Arena, mere kilometers from Tarawa, Bataan, and Corregidor, places known heretofore only from headlines in the newspaper.

On the way to the troop carrier, which had just set down, Gillian met up with Lil, who blew a stream of smoke from her endless supply of Luckys. "You okay?" she asked.

"Good as can be expected," Lil responded. She drew a fake fox wrap around her shoulders and blew another stream of smoke. "Nothing like a little gunfire and blackout curtains to perk a girl up. But I'm sure you have much more to do than wonder about me. I'm fine, just fine. Really."

"Right. And I'm Grover Cleveland's uncle." Gilly stepped up her pace to keep up with Lil. "Look. Why don't we have a cup of joe tomorrow. We can talk about —"

"Sure, Pettibone. Whatever you want." Without waiting for Gilly to finish, Lil pushed ahead of her and started up the boarding stairs, flicking her half-smoked Lucky behind her.

The Musi-Gals boarded the plane single file and took seats on the hard benches lining both sides of the fuselage while the crew stowed their gear. Without any formality whatsoever, the group was soon aloft and headed for Manila.

Gillian and Anna sat side by side, a huge canvas bag of mail strapped onto the bench beside them. Missy, eyes rounded in anticipation, sat on the other side of the bag. Across the narrow aisle, Lil flipped through a dog-eared pulp novel with one hand while grasping the leather strap hanging from the ceiling with the other. The rest of the Musi-Gals had taken seats up and down the fuselage. All were experiencing fear of flying in varying degrees. For many it was the first airplane ride. Anticipation, esprit de corps, and queasy bellies mingled in the small craft.

When the plane leveled off, out the tiny windows could be seen glorious sunshine and brilliant blue sky; below them was the soft gray mattress of the fog bank. "Ya'll doin' okay?" a serviceman asked from the door leading to the cockpit. "Yeah," everyone chorused. "That's good," the airman said. "We might run into some heavy weather later on. Best get your snooze time in now. If our radar is right, there's a real doozy up ahead."

Everyone exchanged glances, searching for reassurance that the Musi-Gals were exempt from such an occurrence. Gillian sat straighter and smiled and nodded at those who looked to her for all to be well. Anna straightened as well and, characteristically, jutted her chin as though defying the very notion of a mishap.

Gillian peered out the window, moved by the flash of sun on the plane's silver wings and the incredible blue of the sky. What harm could come on such a beautiful day? Someone near the rear of the plane yelled out, "Hey, let's sing something." Gillian groaned. "Please, not the beer bottle song again."

"Okay, then, let's jam," Betse sang out. The instruments that had been carried aboard were hastily taken from battered cases. After a short tuning session, the band broke into a song. Gillian and Anna sang along, "You've got to accen-tu-ate the positive . . ." The band jammed while the plane droned on. Some crewmembers standing in the hatchway snapped their fingers and sang along. As time passed, the band grew sleepy. One by one they stopped playing and fell into a light doze. Gillian and Anna fell asleep too, with Anna's head falling to rest on Gillian's shoulder. Only Sue Ellen continued strumming a few chords on her ukelele.

A loud bang sounded and then a clatter as objects fell to the metal floor from overhead storage racks.

An earsplitting whine followed as the plane's engines screamed for altitude. Everyone woke at once. "Wha' the —" Betse yelled. "Oh my god," Lil said piercingly. In an instant the trip had turned ugly. The aircraft screamed higher only to slam into an air pocket, fall, then rise again and rock from side to side.

The plane leveled off at a higher altitude but continued to buck and rock with no sign of letup. The faces on the band members ran the gamut from green to stark white. Instinctively, Gillian reached over and pulled Anna close to her; with her free hand she took Anna's hand and held it firmly.

The plane continued its treacherous bouncing and heaving, but in Gillian's world all the tumult had receded. Anna squeezed her hand hard, and Gillian could feel Anna's breath on her neck, just above her collar. Gillian knew her face was glowing scarlet but figured no one was about to notice. For one crazy instant she wished the plane would buck and spin and rock all the way to Manila.

Anna varied the pressure of her hands in Gilly's, then brought her arm around so that she encircled Gilly's waist. Lightning flashed again and again outside the window; booming thunder followed.

"Gilly," Anna said softly, moving her lips closer to Gillian's ear. "Gilly, I have to tell you something." She held Gillian tighter and whispered, "If we are going to die, there's something I want you to know."

"Yes?" Gillian said hoarsely, afraid her ragged breathing would betray her.

"I love you, Gilly."

Sure her ears had betrayed her, Gilly swallowed hard, grateful for all the noise in the plane so that Anna wouldn't hear the loud gulping sound she made. All of a sudden she felt she didn't need a plane in order to fly. She tried to speak, but the words got stuck. It was okay. She could die now and know she'd had a perfect life. Still, her throat felt tight, and words pushed against her Adam's apple but couldn't get out.

"Like *in* love. Like being in love." Anna placed a soft kiss on Gilly's neck.

I don't want this storm to end, Gillian thought wildly. *Dear god, let this airplane bounce and shudder forever.* "Anna," Gillian gulped, "Anna, I feel the same way. I have for a long time. I just didn't know what to say. I've never felt anything like this before."

"Me neither," Anna said softly into Gilly's neck, "but I like it."

It seemed that the plane's course became smooth, the scream of the engines quieted, and the wild bucking and shaking grew gentle. "We've made it through the worst of it," a soldier yelled from the cockpit. "Hang on, though. We're not out of the woods yet." A few minutes later the flight was calm and smooth, even though they were flying through thick and curdled clouds. Crew and band alike joined in heartfelt applause.

A gigantic mailbag had fallen to the floor, partially obscuring Gillian and Anna. Gillian vowed she would strike a bargain with the devil before letting go of Anna's hand. Apparently, Anna felt much the same, for she made no move to let go of Gillian. Amid relieved whoops, loud chanting prayers to the deity, and ultimately a rousing chorus of "Praise the Lord and pass the ammunition," Gillian and Anna remained silent.

They dared not look at one another as that

seemed far too dangerous, especially in so small a plane with their friends packed tightly around them. Anna got up to go the loo, but as soon as she returned she again grasped Gillian's hand, which rested on the bench seat beside her, and held it throughout the long flight to Manila.

At midnight, the plane landed at its destination. The camp was in almost total darkness; only a few dim flares lit the runway. Looking out the window, Gillian saw her first ever coconut palm tree. Someone opened the hatchway almost immediately and instructed the women to walk, single file, through the pitch-black night, moving to their immediate left. Someone would be waiting.

The women did as they were told and almost bumped into a lanky sergeant who held a flashlight covered with some kind of cloth. "This way," he said. "Just a few more steps." Soon the troupe walked through the door to a darkened Quonset hut, pulled aside the blackout curtain, and saw low lights for the first time since landing. "These are your quarters," the sergeant said. "Make yourselves at home."

Two kerosene lanterns, one at either end of the hut, cast eerie shadows over the army-issue cots and along the walls and the rounded tin ceiling. The room was bare of any furnishings other than the wooden clothes lockers between each cot. Mosquito netting cascaded from an overhead ring above each narrow, thin bed.

"Home indeed," Missy yelped.

Betse called back, "Well, the Carlton it ain't. But

I'm so tired I could sleep on a bed of nails. Who's first in the bathroom?"

"It's called a *latrine,* dummy. And nobody gets to be first," Lil called. "There're fifteen sinks and fifteen potties in there. No waiting, ladies, step right up."

Gillian stood by the door making sure everyone was accounted for. She spoke briefly with the sergeant about mess times and where they should report the following morning. He answered all her questions, then said, "Say, we've really been looking forward to your show. A bunch of guys who've just seen action are here, and what an audience they'll turn out to be. See you all at reveille."

"Glad we are able to do our part, soldier," Gillian said while peering over his shoulder into the dim interior of the Quonset looking for Anna. She found her, in the last cot on the left, just beside the latrine.

Anna's face wore a look of abject disappointment. She shrugged her shoulders and mouthed something about trying to save the cot next to hers. But Betse had taken up residence on one side of her, while Marge was nearly asleep in her cot on the other.

Gillian struggled for control, afraid of her own bitter disappointment. She walked over to Anna's cot. "My teeth feel like they're wearing sweaters," she blurted. "Wanna go wash up?" In the latrine she and Anna stood at the sinks. Through a mouthful of toothpaste Gillian glanced at Anna and whispered, "Let's meet first thing in the morning, just after reveille. I've got to talk to you." She smiled, uncaring of the toothpaste rounding her full lips.

"I'll be there," Anna whispered. "And I'll be wearing those proverbial bells."

Gillian woke early the following morning drenched in sweat. There wasn't a hint of a breeze, and through the window, now cleared of blackout curtains, the sun blazed mercilessly. Her sheet felt damp and sticky. All of it gave her a headache, including the fact she had spent a restless night. Thoughts of Anna and her breath on Gillian's neck, the kiss, the very words both had spoken wouldn't let her sleep. So many thoughts and feelings had collided in Gillian's heart and head that she awoke feeling as though she had been tossed into her mother's old Mixmaster.

Great god almighty! She had never felt so good in all her life. The promises of all the ballads she loved so dearly were finally coming to pass. The wrinkle occurred when Gillian thought about the fact that Anna was a woman. Had what happened between them been some sort of a freak accident? Had this ever happened to anyone else? Surely Lil hadn't meant the sweet love she felt for Anna when she had hissed the word *dyke* in her face in Milwaukee.

Gillian was more blissful than frightened by her midnight ruminations. She got up before anyone else, dressed quietly, and went to the mess tent for coffee and a few moments to think before Anna showed up.

Idly she thought about the boy she had dated for a time in high school, the one who had almost rubbed her shoulder raw in his awkward attempt at petting. She had, back then, felt only indifference and irritation. *Indifference* was hardly the word to describe her feelings this blast furnace-hot morning sitting in front of the mess tent somewhere in the Philippines.

Gilly lit another Lucky and sat smoking and drinking coffee, her red hair ablaze in the morning sun. Since their clothes still had not arrived, she had dressed in khaki trousers, an army green T-shirt and, as directed, in combat boots — to insure against biting insects and unwary snakes, the quartermaster had explained. She took a long pull on the Lucky, tilted her head, and blew a huge stream of smoke toward heaven.

A whiff of a breeze raised a strand or two of her hair and at the same time dislodged a coconut from the tree just behind her. The coconut rolled to a stop at her feet. She picked it up and examined it. She had never before seen a real coconut, only the shredded kind in cellophane packs her mother bought for her Sunday coconut cake. It looked like anything but what it was. The coconut was brown, stringy, and unpleasant looking on the outside, belying the tender, sweet meat on the inside. The incongruity struck Gilly as funny. She threw back her head and laughed aloud, tossing the coconut repeatedly into the air. "You can't judge a book, etcetera," she laughed with each catch.

A serviceman strolled by and whistled. Gilly missed her catch, and the coconut fell to the ground. "Say. You're one of them USO dames, aint'cha?" he called. Gilly nodded lamely, feeling less like a dame than anything else she could possibly imagine.

She sat back on the bench and crossed her legs, swinging her booted foot even more vigorously than before. What did Anna feel like this morning? A rush of fear knocked Gilly to a full upright position, both boots planted in the dirt. Well, what did Anna feel? Maybe she slept the whole thing off and this morning would be just business as usual. Maybe Anna felt afraid now and wouldn't want to see Gilly at all. "Well, I'm afraid too," Gilly muttered, already angry at what had not happened. "Me, too." For emphasis she kicked the dropped coconut. "I'm scared because nothing like this has ever happened to me. I love you, Anna McGraw. That's it. Just like that. Plain and simple." Gilly hopped around the bench, muttering words she hoped no one else could hear. "And, here's the really important thing. I don't want to lose you. Not for any reason. I'm not upset because you're a woman. Hell, I'm tickled pink."

Gilly didn't so much see Anna come down the whitewashed stone path as she sensed a presence behind her. She whirled around. Anna stood there, more beautiful than any creature alive and dressed in the same garb as Gilly, except Anna had pinned her hair at each temple with metal barrettes in the shape of bluebirds. Gilly, who had worked herself into quite a froth, faced Anna with wild, dancing eyes and hair like Roman candles at dusk. "Hi," Anna said, smiling softly.

"Hi," Gilly said, attempting to compose herself. There was a short silence. Gilly tucked her T-shirt into her trousers. She grinned at Anna.

"Hi," Anna said again. This time dropping her eyes slightly.

"Hi, yourself," Gilly repeated. Gilly only thought she had felt fear in the past. Now she feared her heart might burst through her chest, and that fear took her breath away.

"I'm glad to see you," Anna said. Her eyes were soft and bright.

Gilly, still fearful her heart might plop out on the ground, managed, "Me, too."

"Let's take a walk," Anna said and slipped her hand into the crook of Gilly's elbow.

"Yes, yes. To someplace a bit more private. But don't you want coffee first?"

"No," Anna said, her cheeks inflamed, her eyes large and moist. "I don't need a thing this morning except a nice long walk with you." With that she exerted the tiniest pressure on Gilly's arm, and they floated away in the general direction of a clump of coconut trees.

Beyond the clump of trees lay a long sandy beach. Gilly took off her heavy boots in order to feel the soft warmth of the sand. Anna followed suit and, holding hands, they began walking. Neither spoke. Gilly felt as though she were tilted, walking kind of slantwise, or floating. At even the slightest movement or change of pressure of Anna's hand in hers, she was overcome with a sharp, sweet belly stab of passion.

Anna's face glowed bright and dewy; every time Gilly stole a quick look at her, she thought her insides would surely melt. Never had she seen so sweet a sight as Anna's hair just where the bluebird barrettes held it. She wished she could draw or paint or compose a poem about the sweetness in just that one tiny bit of Anna.

Instead she leaned over and kissed the spot, lightly but as though drinking it up. Anna stopped walking and turned her face toward the kiss, sliding to meet Gilly's lips. Their lips lingered together, shyly for a moment, exploring. In that same moment the world turned mute. The South China Sea vanished. The birds and the beach all vanished, along with reason and thought. The world as they had known it vanished then and there, dissolved by soft moans and ragged breathing as each woman found, in the form and flesh of the other, first love.

Anna broke the kiss and buried her face in Gilly's shoulder. Her breath came in short pants, and the feeling of Anna's breathing against Gilly's neck stirred Gilly to a depth she never knew existed.

"Oh, Gilly, I was so afraid," Anna said. "I've felt this way about you almost from the first time I saw you on that train platform. I didn't know what to do. Nothing like this has, well, ever happened to me." Anna shivered and held Gilly more tightly. "I was so afraid that if I said anything, or did anything, you might bolt. I wasn't able to tolerate the thought that we might not see each other ever again."

"Anna," Gilly tried to speak but her voice seemed out of control, coming out of her as a squeak. "I know, I know. Sometimes I thought my heart would burst if I looked at you just one more time," Gilly managed. "But it all seemed so dangerous. I mean, this isn't your ordinary boy-meets-girl story. I didn't want you to hate me."

"Hate you!" Anna tossed her head and laughed, parting lips red and full with passion. "Oh, love, how could I ever hate you. I love you. God, how I love you."

They embraced again and Gilly said, "Isn't it awful we each had to think the worst of what we were feeling. It's not fair. It's not right."

"I don't think the world out there is going to be all that thrilled for us," Anna said, "but I don't care. Not one whit do I care. We've found each other, and that's all that matters to me."

"Do you think anyone else has ever felt like this? Surely this has happened to other women?" Anna asked.

"Oh, sure, I've heard stories. But I always thought it was like, well, like some weird thing that happened to a few women who dressed like men, some sort of kinky sexual thing. I've heard about that sort of thing, but that's not us, Anna. I don't feel weird at all. Just happier than I have a right to be, or that anyone has a right to be," Gilly smiled.

"You know what, Gilly? I'm sure if everyone knew how happy we are, how much it means to find a true love, if others could truly see our happiness they would be thrilled for us. It's not every day one finds love. I'd like to shout our love from the rooftops."

"My better judgment cautions otherwise." Gilly laughed and hugged Anna to her.

"You're right, of course. We can do no such thing. Ours will have to be a private joy. But in my heart I'm singing from every rooftop in sight."

They began walking again, slowly. "There are so many ways I want to touch you," Gilly said. "So many ways I want to feel you next to me."

"Yes. I can't keep my mouth or hands off you. I don't want to stop touching you."

"But not here. Not now," Gilly rasped. "We will meet here tonight after the show. Just you and me and the moon."

"We better head back right now," Anna said. "If we stay out here much longer I'm not responsible for my actions."

They reached the clump of palms from which they had descended to the beach and knelt to lace up their boots. Gilly saw a quick flash of movement and looked up to see Lil. She was standing half hidden among the trees. Gilly's throat tightened, and her body trembled. Still, she managed her voice and called out, "Hello, Lil."

Lil ambled toward them, her face quizzical but unsmiling. "Hi, girls," she said. "Just came down to get a view of the water and saw you two coming along the beach headed this way."

"Yeah," Anna said quickly. "You should take a walk down there. It's very special."

"Maybe I just will," Lil replied, "since you recommend it so highly." She pulled her hair from her eyes to drape behind one ear and walked stiffly past, turning one last look at Gilly with Anna at her side before disappearing down the path to the beach.

"Oh my god," Gilly moaned as soon as they were out of earshot. "Do you suppose she saw us?"

"No, I don't think so. If she'd seen us kissing she would have had the entire Fourth Army down here to gape. She'd be on the phone to Nolan Phelps getting us fired this very minute."

"Yes, I suppose. But I get the feeling she was

snooping. We have to be very careful. We have to be on guard so nothing ugly ever touches us."

Anna gave her assent with a strong squeeze of Gilly's hand before dropping it as they reached the military compound. The place was swarming.

"It's almost time for rehearsal," Gilly said. "You go on in, and I'll wait a few minutes. That way no one will see us coming in together."

"Honestly, Gilly. Do you think that's necessary?"

"I don't know what's necessary and what's not. I just can't stand to think of anyone prying into something that is entirely our business."

Anna scurried toward the huge mess tent patting her hair in place and returning her shirttail to the waistband of her trousers. Gilly smiled and took the long way around, striding through several rows of barracks before going in to meet up with the others. She decided to call a very short rehearsal. The performance that night would likely be long, loud, and rowdy, and she didn't want to get tired. There was a whole lot more to look forward to than rehearsals and performances.

True to her intuition, the night's performance was a long and jubilant one. The Musi-Gals had never sounded better. Never had she and Anna sung the familiar words to the songs as they did on this night. They crooned and belted them out, perspiring heavily under the lights and grinning like fools at the audience, the band, and each other. Feeling the music as never before, they happily performed five encores without the slightest let up of steam, ending finally with "Chattanooga Choo Choo." The audience of GIs, even then, whooped and howled for more, but Gilly and Anna had exchanged a glance and a nod, signaling that the music and the words required a far different means of expression, and the sooner they were off the stage, the better.

It wasn't necessary to strike the stage for the night as the concert was held in an unused plane hangar, the same location that would be used every night of their gig there. When the concert and the applause were finally over, a line of jeeps appeared to carry the weary musicians back to their Quonset.

Everyone had felt the excitement of the performance, and all but Gilly and Anna chalked it up to the thrill of their first real war-zone concert. The several jeep loads of ballyhooing, laughing women crept to a stop, and the Musi-Gals fell out of the jeeps jostling, laughing, and calling to one another. Gilly thought the whole process excruciatingly long and kept wondering how long it would take before the group finally cooled down and went to sleep.

She and Anna made a point of socializing and joking with other members of the band. Even so, Gilly was as aware of Anna's presence as if she had been wired to her by some magical lover's radar. Occasionally they stole glances but were careful to moderate the longing and the love that poured from their expressions.

It was well after two in the morning when Anna, who had been feigning sleep, rose from her cot and made her way through the darkened hut in the direction of the latrine. Gilly lay still, waiting and listening. Only deep silence, punctuated now and then by the low sounds of sleep, filled the Quonset. Quietly she got up and followed Anna to the back of the hut. Anna waited for her in a small hallway. Beyond the hallway was an exit, and beyond that the freedom of a dark and starless night.

It was hot out, and steamy. Anna more or less led the way to the clump of palm trees and the beach beyond. They moved quickly, avoiding the gravel paths so that crunching sounds wouldn't give away their presence. The entire camp was asleep. There were sentries at the main gates and along the boundary fencing, but neither had seen a sentry post during their earlier walk on the beach. They approached the deserted mess area and veered right toward the trees.

"Halt! Who goes there?" As sudden as that, a figure loomed in front of them, a muscular man wearing a white helmet and holding a rifle with a fixed bayonet. Shocked, Gilly stood rigidly in the sand wishing she knew what to do next. The man approached from the shadows, and as he came closer Anna called out, "Hi there. It's only us." If she was as frightened as Gilly, her voice did not betray her. She sounded light, lilting, even nonchalant.

"Oh, hi there, ladies," the beefy soldier said easily. "Didn't know it was you. Say, great show you did tonight. We just about ate it up."

"That's sweet news, soldier," Anna spoke again. "We aim to please. But say, how about pointing that thing somewhere else?" she gestured toward the rifle still aimed at her chest.

"Oh, sure. Sorry. 'Scuse me, ma'am. I'm just surprised to see you up and about so late."

It was Gilly's turn to say something. "You know how it is, soldier. Too much excitement from the concert. Just couldn't sleep and thought we'd take a short stroll on the beach. Maybe after that we can grab some shut-eye."

"That's jake with me. Must be tough to relax after a show. And you were really jivin', eight to the bar." He waggled his forefinger in the air. "Go on. I think it's pretty safe down there. But just so you won't worry, I'll be up here looking out for ya. Won't let no lonely soldiers down on the beach tonight. Have a nice walk. Sure won't miss your show tomorrow night."

They crept soundlessly down to the beach and were several feet away before they began to giggle. "You were great, Anna. You just answered right up like we were out for just an ordinary little walk at two in the morning."

"Well, aren't we? I mean, what more ordinary thing for lovers to do than have a late night stroll on the beach?" Anna tossed her head and stuck out her chin. Grinning, she took hold of Gilly's hand and pulled her along. "I would have loved to flounce away from there, you know, something sweeping and grand."

"Why didn't you?" Gilly asked, her trust in Anna growing with each passing moment.

"It's hard to flounce properly in army-issue T-shirts and fatigues. C'mon."

Far down the beach they found a small inlet where a fresh water stream made its way to the sea.

There was a low curving bluff and vegetation from small, stunted trees. They walked up the streambed a few paces and, finally satisfied that no one in the world knew their whereabouts, fell to the sand in an embrace. Kisses and moans and half words steamed between them.

Profound passion did not require haste, and each woman thrilled to new and newer heights at the graze of a breast against an arm or the exquisite ache at the beginnings of a new kiss. There was nothing that should be missed in the knowing of each other, nothing to hurry the exploration and the careful tending of so huge a passion.

At the edge of the precipice, even before lips and fingers explored the sweet openings and crevices of love, still there was no hurry. Each separate pang, each separate tremor, demanded its own time and its own life. Finally, one extra spark, a moan, a spasm too many, a breath against an ear broke the dam, and the passion boiled over, steaming and frothing unchecked.

They lay back on the sandy ground. Gilly, far beyond words, felt the errant contractions of spent passion roll on and on in the deepest part of her belly. They lay for a time staring up at the stars and listening to the waves break against the shore. Neither spoke; words were needless in the wake of so magnificent a communion.

When at last Gilly felt she had regained enough of her body to speak and move, she lit cigarettes for each of them, passing one to Anna and blowing out a long stream of smoke. She took Anna's hand and held it, caressing Anna's palm with the tips of her fingers, astounded by the quick fire of renewed passion.

They made love again, holding tightly to each other, trying to suppress the yelps and groans of passion, sometimes crushing their mouths together to hold in the sounds of desire.

At last they dressed and crept quietly back to the Quonset hut, arms around the other. Gilly wiped her hankie across her face. As she suspected, there was moisture there, moisture from her happy tears.

Ten

After several weeks at Camp Pershing, the musical ensemble and the lead singers settled into a routine of rehearsals and performances and felt less like strangers in their exotic new home. Gilly and Anna's love affair continued, but the strain of secrecy was telling on them.

The schedule was grueling. Sometimes there were two performances a day, and several times a week the band was flown to surrounding islands for even more performances. The heat was stifling and the mosquitoes rampant. The little time left after shows and rehearsals was devoted to the daily routines of washing hair, doing laundry, and going on little shopping trips in Manila. A group of men from Special Services made a recording of their show to sell at the PX and had plans to sell the album to a label in the United States for distribution there.

Gilly and Anna continued to meet at night after everyone else had gone to sleep. The sentry called them by name and each time complimented them on the night's show and wished them a nice stroll. He seemed a little in awe of them and pleased to humor the eccentricities of performing artists.

Early one sweaty morning, Gilly strolled back to the Quonset after breakfast, plopped on her bed, and announced there would be no rehearsal that day. Whoops of approval filled the hut. Everyone was tired and needed a break, especially Gilly, who had not had a decent night's sleep in weeks. Immediate plans got underway for a shopping trip in the afternoon to the stores in Manila. Some of the other band members had ventured into the town and had returned with tales of all the hard-to-get items packed on the shelves of local merchants. Nylons and lipstick could be had for a song.

"C'mon, Pettibone. You up to it?" Missy sat on the cot across from Gilly. "Say, you're not looking so good, kiddo. You've got a lot of extra baggage under those eyelids. You okay?"

"Yeah, yeah. I'm fine. It's probably just the heat." Gilly squirmed inside. Even so innocent an observation as Missy's could cause her heart to race.

She glanced over at Anna, standing a few feet away, to see if she had overheard. Anna smiled but kept talking to Betse and Lil about the shopping trip.

Within a few hours all had boarded one of the shuttles that ran from the base into the city. Gilly made a point of sitting next to someone else. Spilling out onto the street and in among the numerous shops, Anna and Gilly laughed and joked with the others and secretly thrilled at chance touchings and furtive glances.

In one shop where a clump of women stood together at a counter, Anna suddenly seized a satin pillow with rose tassels from a bin of many similar pillows. The pillow was pink and blue with a map of the Philippines on one side. She held it aloft and headed for the cashier. "I'll take this one. It's exactly what I need."

Later on the ride back to the base, Gilly and Anna sat together. Gilly asked, "What was all the excitement about that pillow? There must be a ton of them in every shop in Manila."

"It's for us, sweetie. We need it for our little late-night beach parties," Anna grinned devilishly.

Gilly blushed and scooted a hair closer to Anna on the bus seat. "You wicked, wicked woman. I hope you live to be a hundred. And me too. Maybe by then I'll grow tired of you."

"I can see it now. There we are racing our wheelchairs toward each other for a night of whoopee. Pretty risqué, don't you think? I hope it all comes true."

"Oh, it will. I have a theory about longevity. See, I think women live longer than men for a very specific reason."

"Yeah? And what might that be, professor?"

"Because we sit down to pee."

Anna guffawed. "Gilly. You are the strangest, most —"

"No. I'm serious. Just think about it a minute. If you added up all the extra minutes of rest we get in a lifetime — and I mean sitting-down, off-your-dogs rest — then my theory makes perfect sense. I've never calculated it, but I'll bet all that rest could add up to years."

Still laughing, Anna slipped her arm through the crook of Gilly's elbow. "I'm the luckiest woman alive. Not only will I live to be ancient, but I'll get to do it with you."

Later that night Gilly and Anna traveled the familiar path to the beach. A breeze had blown up, and they walked quickly, bent forward slightly at the waist. Anna clutched the shiny new pillow in front of her.

After they made love they lay quietly in each other's arms and stared through the bower of branches at a full, lush moon. Gilly began to fidget, and her breathing became uneven. Anna, thinking of more passion, turned toward her. She kissed Gilly's neck. Instead of responding, Gilly leapt to her feet and began to pace. Anna pulled on her shirt and went to Gilly, who by now had started wading in the shallow surf.

Anna tucked her arm through Gilly's and walked quietly along beside her for a while. "What's up, chum?" she finally asked, her shirttail billowing behind her in the breeze, her breasts translucent in the moonlight. Gilly wanted to brush off the question, respond with a dismissive shrug. She wanted to go back to their private little cove and begin making love all over again. But there was a problem, a dark uneasiness growing up inside her. She'd been sensing it for days, tormenting herself whether what she sensed was real or merely a projection of her fear that she and Anna would be found out. She felt sure Lil knew, or at least suspected — the strange looks, the smirks, the way Lil had begun watching her and watching Anna too. It was like Lil was looking for something.

Gilly threw her arm around Anna's shoulder and steered her toward the lights of the camp. "C'mon, hon. Let's get back. I just feel a bit jumpy tonight. Maybe it's lack of sleep." She winked at Anna and tugged her quickly along the moonwashed strand. As they neared the well-trodden path leading away from the beach, Anna removed her arm from Gilly's waist and gently massaged her back.

"I think I can guess what you're thinking," she said and gave Gilly's shoulder a soft shake. "I'm no mind reader, but I think I've gotten to know you pretty well, my sweet. If it helps any, just please know this. If anything, and I mean *anything,* happens to us because of what we are to each other, well, I just want you to know that I will never leave you. Not ever. Not for anything."

"I love you so much, Anna," Gilly breathed. "I can't bear to think of anyone making something ugly out of what we are to each other. I'll fight, too, of course. But, there're only two of us and so many Philistines out there. I wish we could just go away someplace and never have to worry about the what-ifs."

"Maybe we can someday, after the war is over."

"Oh, we will. We'll find a place where no one can hurt us and we can be ourselves. If anything sullies what we've found, it would be like crankcase oil poured over a piece of fine French lace. I just won't let it happen." Gilly spat out these words and raised her fist to the darkening night. "I won't. I swear it."

The following day was Sunday, and no concert was scheduled. Gilly awoke to the blessed knowledge that sleeping late was at last an option. She tried to ban consciousness and return to sleep, but she was aware of a low, rattling sound that soon turned into a loud pounding on the tin roof of the Quonset hut. It was raining. *Good.* She tried to bury deeper into the round wool army blanket. Instead of blaring heat and light at the windows, the view this morning was of sheeting rain slamming against the glass panes.

Gilly stretched lazily on the narrow cot, luxuriating in the extra hours of rest. The barracks were quiet. The other women snored or turned softly in sleep. A few were awake and talking quietly. Someone was brushing her teeth on the other side of the pressboard partition. Until now Gilly had not realized just how tired out she really was, how those nights of lovemaking after the concerts had taken their toll. *God, what a luxury sleep is,* she thought.

Through the fog of a deepening sleep, Gilly heard her name called. A husky male voice yelled, "Miss Pettibone. Pettibone. Front and center, please." She crawled out of bed wiping the sleep from her eyes. A glance at her watch told her it was past eleven in the morning. She stumbled toward the Quonset's door shaking her head to rid the cobwebs. "Damn," she mouthed. "Sleep. I want sleep."

A young private stood in the open doorway, his olive slicker glistening with sheets of rain. " 'Scuse me, ma'am, but the commandant wants to see you. Says it's urgent. Would you follow me, please."

Gilly dressed quickly and followed the young man into the rain. They slogged through puddles of water, and rain poured through the collar of Gilly's olive drab slicker. "This better be good," she muttered aloud, wishing she were back in her dry bunk sleeping and dreaming of Anna.

Headquarters was alive with lights and movement. Jeeps sluiced through deep ravines of water outside, and uniformed men walked briskly about the daily business of the army inside. Gilly entered the building and shook herself in the doorway, sending water flying in all directions. "The commandant's office is this way," her escort said. Gilly followed him through a wide doorway into the flag-draped office of the commander of the Camp Pershing Operations.

"Pettibone?" The commander asked without smiling, his lips set firmly in a flushed face.

"Right," Gilly answered and started to take a seat at the huge desk.

"No need to take a seat, Miss Pettibone. This will be short and to the point. I'm in possession of a wire from Nolan Phelps at the USO headquarters ordering you and your band back to the U.S. Your tour of duty here has been cancelled." The commander spat these words at Gilly, his face becoming darker as he spoke.

"I'm sorry. I'm afraid I don't understand. Cancelled?"

"That's right, Pettibone. Cancelled. And, damned good riddance, too, if you ask me."

Gilly's knees turned to jelly. She felt her breath catch in her throat as she sank into a chair beside his desk. "But, Commander, I don't understand," she managed.

"Oh, c'mon. Sure you do. You didn't think you could have a lezzie affair right under the nose of the U.S. Army, did you? If you did you're sicker than I think, Pettibone. And here's another thing. Just to show you we won't tolerate this filthy abomination, you and your girlfriend have just one hour to pack up and be on a transport plane out of here. The rest of the band will leave on a later plane."

Gilly felt frozen in a nightmare, as if the world outside had vanished and she would spend an eternity immobilized in torment. The room spun and she wrapped her arms around her middle tightly so as to remain seated and not fly apart at the seams. "But, how did you — uh, I mean, who told you this?" Her voice sounded strange, like it came from somewhere else, someone else.

"I probably shouldn't tell you this, but our informant is one of your own. A member of your little band. We're proud of her for having the decency to speak out about this, this filth."

"Lil," Gilly whispered. It had to have been Lil. But why? How could she have known? Gilly felt as if she were crumbling into a million pieces. And Anna, how could she protect Anna from this horrible experience? Sweat poured from Gilly's forehead; her hands trembled as she rose and pulled her slicker tightly around her. "Don't I have a right to a reply?" Gilly asked. Maybe, if there was a chance to deny everything, they could at least get out of this horrible place without everyone knowing. God, what a mess. The last thing on earth Gilly wanted to do was deny her love for Anna. No. The last thing was to have their relationship, so loving, so sweet, dragged through the mud of other people's hatred.

"No," the commander replied quickly. "All we need to send you packing is the accusation. You know, where there's smoke, and so on. If you were army, we'd know what to do with you, and it wouldn't be pretty. But since you are civilian, we're just getting you the hell out of the way of all decent human beings. You're dismissed, Pettibone. Be on that transport plane in one hour."

Gilly started toward the door, walking in a trance, neither feeling her feet on the floor nor seeing through her tear-clouded eyes.

"Just one more thing, Pettibone," the commander called, his voice oozing sarcasm. "Just how do two girls do it anyway? I always heard you use Coke bottles for a dick."

Long after Gilly had slammed the door and started toward the Quonset hut where Anna waited, the commander's remark sliced through her very soul. Her fear waned as anger built inside her. What right had he to speak so filthy a remark? What right had anyone to judge the love she bore for Anna, and Anna for her? Gilly's tears of shock and fear were replaced by tears of anger.

She reached for the door then hesitated. No one, especially Anna, should see her like this. She needed time to compose herself. She turned and started walking into the rain, headed toward the beach. Her mind, though numbed by the ugly scene in the commandant's office, now held only one thought. Anna. What would she say? What would Anna do now that their relationship had been trashed, like so much garbage? Gilly felt a fresh onslaught of tears flood her eyes. She placed her hands over her face and wept. Tears and rain streamed down her face in a river of despair.

"Anna. Oh, Anna, I'm so sorry," Gilly sobbed. "I would have done anything to protect you from this."

"I know, sweet. And I you." Anna laid a hand on Gilly's shoulder.

Gilly whirled around at Anna's calming voice. "What are you doing here? Oh, Anna. Something awful has happened. The commandant —"

"Yes, I know. I know everything, my love. The commandant sent a messenger to our Quonset. Everybody knows. We are being shipped stateside."

"Do they know why?"

"Yes, Gilly. They do."

"Oh my god, Anna. Oh my god," Gilly wailed, her face a mask of pain. She felt her heart might stop beating. She heard a high, thin wailing in her ears. "What did you do? How did they treat you?"

"You mean the Musi-Gals? Well, everybody was pretty stunned to say the least — most of 'em, anyway." Anna managed a smile, reaching to brush a strand of wet hair from Gilly's face. She pressed the tendril behind Gilly's ear then softly kissed her cheek, and Gilly did not miss the red-rimmed eyes, the tiny tear that Anna quickly wiped away with her sleeve. "They were struggling for words when I saw you through the door."

"You mean no one said anything nasty? Not even Lil?"

"Some comments were made. But I just got up, flounced to the door, and announced that they should all be so lucky. Half of those babes wouldn't know true love if it jumped up and bit them."

Gilly wanted to fall to her knees with relief. Anna wouldn't fold. Far from it, she seemed to rise to the occasion, showing at this moment more grit and spunk than Gilly. Gilly took a step toward Anna and, after a moment's hesitation, folded her into her arms. "Oh, Anna," she moaned, her face crushed against the nape of Anna's neck. Nothing had ever felt so precious, yet so forbidden and so dangerous. "What would I do without you?"

"That's something you'll not have to find out, my sweet. I promise you." Anna pulled her face away from Gilly to stare at her long and deeply. She kissed her, crushing Gilly's mouth to hers, circling Gilly's trembling body with her arms.

Yet even in the circle of Anna's arms, even as she read in the touch and caress of her lover the assurance she so craved, Gilly's mind and heart screamed. "I hate them!" she moaned, half a cry, half a guttural, feral stab at her tormentors. "We haven't hurt anyone. Why should they care who a person falls in love with? What pompous, sanctimonious people. I'd like to kill somebody. Honest, Anna. I would."

"Hush. Don't talk that way." Anna hugged Gilly harder and stroked her face. "Let them say whatever they will. I don't care. I have something that means more to me than any silly convention, than rules contrived by little minds. I have you. No one and nothing can take that from me. We've been given a gift, a very rare and precious one. Millions of people will live entire lifetimes and never know the kind of love we have together."

"But Anna, don't you see? I've gotten you into this, this horror —"

"Just stop that right now, Gillian Pettibone." Anna held Gilly at arm's length and stared into her face. "First of all, you didn't get me into a thing. I take credit for that myself, thank you very much. I chose *you!* No, let me rephrase that. I *choose* you! Right here. Right now. Come what may." Thunder rolled across the dark sky, and Anna had to shout. "And second, I have no intention of letting this, this nasty little scene separate me from the only true love I have ever known. Got it?"

Gilly smiled weakly and pulled Anna to her. "Where will we go? What will we do? I can't bear the thought of another filthy remark, another insult. What we have is too fine. I can't stand for what we have to be dragged through the muck." Gilly almost wailed, and her tears began afresh. "Oh, Anna. I'm sorry I'm acting like a big baby. It's just that I love you so much. I wanted only good for us."

"Then, by god, that's what we shall have."

Anna held Gilly and continued stroking her face and hair. "Oh, baby. Please don't feel so responsible for everything. Remember, we're in this together. But I am hatching a little plan. Would you like to hear it?" At Gilly's soft nod, Anna chuckled lightly.

"Some years ago my grandmother left me a little nest egg, my mad money she used to call it. I don't think she ever once believed I'd make the grade as a diva, or for that matter, get married. She wanted to see that I had some independence from all the conventions my parents imposed. She was a great lady. I'm sorry you never got to meet her. But I digress. Anyway, there is a nice little trust fund sitting patiently in a bank at home, drawing interest like bees to nectar. We aren't rich by any means, but, we ain't broke either. How do you like them apples?"

For the first time in the savage events of the last hour, Gillian's face brightened a bit. "You don't say? A lady of independent means, eh? That's terrific, Anna. Really it is. But I don't see what good money will do. We'll be pariahs wherever we go. People will say nasty things. In most places, we could be arrested." Gilly slumped like an emptied grain sack and lowered her eyes.

"Money will buy plenty, Miss Pettibone — not love, that's for sure — but it will sure purchase a heap of privacy. For instance, have you ever been to the Northwest? The Olympic peninsula is one of the most beautiful — dare I say, remote — places I've ever visited. C'mon, buckeroo. Buck up. I can't wait to get you into those dark woods all to myself. The big bad wolf has nothing on me." Gilly looked at Anna and saw the familiar smile and the soft brown of her eyes and felt ashamed. How could she have doubted?

Relief and gratitude and love as deep as her heart could reach radiated through her, and she drew Anna closer and kissed her.

A harsh sound and a rough hand on her arm shook Gilly. She opened her eyes to see two white-helmeted MPs standing beside them. "You are under arrest," one of them said. "I'm afraid you'll have to come with us." The other grabbed Anna's arms and held them behind her. He clamped a pair of handcuffs on her just as the other soldier attempted to put handcuffs on Gilly.

"What the hell are you doing?" Gilly screamed. "What are you talking about? Arrested for what?"

One soldier looked down at the ground, embarrassed. The other one spat on the ground, "For being queer. For being dykes, lezzies. What you just did is against the law."

"We hugged," Gilly protested. "I kissed her. Is that against the law?"

"You bet it is, lady. We may be in the Philippines, but as far as you are concerned it might as well be the good old US of A. C'mon. I think you've got a plane to catch." Roughly he pushed Gilly so that she almost tripped into the mud. "Get a move on. The plane is about to leave."

Red-faced and in shock, Gilly and Anna marched handcuffed through the rain, the MPs just behind them. "Take these things off me," Gilly demanded. "Believe me, I have no wish to be anywhere but on that plane."

"No chance, doll," one of the soldiers said and pushed her again. She almost lost her balance in the slippery mud, but Anna steadied her.

Knots of soldiers stood in the rain all along the route Anna and Gilly walked to the plane. Some of them jeered and made catcalls. "Queers." "Diesel dykes." Others only stared at them, mouths set in thin lines, appearing angry and embarrassed that they had applauded them and clapped and whistled for more. Some of the Musi-Gals were scattered among the men, and when Anna and Gilly passed they averted their eyes. Missy and Sue Ellen burst into tears.

Into the yawning maw of pain and humiliation, Gilly scarcely felt she had room to feel the shame of letting the band down — after all their hard work. But as she saw the band standing silently in the rain, she felt tears wash again to her eyes. "Oh my god," she groaned, "please, get me into that plane."

Just as they approached the gangway, the commandant, who had been watching the spectacle from a palm-thatched hut, strode toward them. "Remove those cuffs," he ordered. Staring at them as the MP removed the handcuffs from each arm, he spat on the ground. "All I want from the likes of you is just to get the hell out of my sight and off the property of the United States Army. You're a disgrace to the uniform and to everything we are fighting for. The last goddamn thing I need is for you two lezzies to spew your sickness all over the courts of the US of A. I'd rather fuck a nip than have anyone stateside think we had harbored a couple of sicko chicks at Pershing. Just get on that plane and out of here. Where you go and what you do is none of my concern after you're out of here and morale has been restored. Now, march!"

At 0800 hours, the small plane was aloft and breaking through thick clouds over the South China Sea. The only passengers sat silent as the wings dipped toward the west. They held hands tightly, and neither looked out of the small windows for a last look.

The End
of the Story

Eleven

A soft, agreeable time remained before dark. Gilly stood at one of the long windows in the parlor staring into a soft shaft of light.

She was particularly intent on the many motes of dust in the light and how they reminded her of what music looked like inside her head when she had played the saxophone.

Anna had spent the better part of the afternoon playing in a bed of tea roses. In that there was no breeze, Gilly knew Anna was still out there by the soft shiver and sway of the delicate roses. The blossoms reminded her of a large basketful of spilled guest soaps — ornate, expensive, and perfumed.

She turned from the window and took another long look at the interior of the house. It sparkled. The painter had long since finished, and every surface gleamed with a new coat of buttery white. And there was more. Just a little after sunrise, a telephone man had visited the house and, with gadgets jingling from his belt, had installed what Anna and she assumed was a phone, although it didn't resemble anything they had seen before. To begin with, the instrument was much too small and defied all practicality. Then there was the business of what happened when it rang at midday.

Neither spirit had been all that disturbed at first. After all, there is nothing menacing about a ringing phone, except perhaps the irritation. But when it was answered? Now, that was something to be reckoned with. Both heard the phone as it was picked up and answered by an unseen voice. Their first thought was to look about, assuming that another spirit had found her way inside.

But that was as much nonsense as an invisibly answered phone. No one ever came there, dead *or* alive. Not since that miserable pair had moved out ever so long ago.

Startled, they stared at the mysterious machine and its disembodied voice. A woman's voice, calm and self-assured, spoke. "Hi. This is Ellie. Neither Tessa nor I are in right now, but do leave a message. If you're calling about a reservation, please let us know the best time to reach you. You may leave your message at the beep. Thanks."

Less than a flash later another voice. "Hey, girls. Just checking in. I wanted to make sure you were bearing up out there in the wilds and to pass on a hot news flash. Dateline Seattle. I have fallen in love! Really! And this time it's forever. I can't wait to see you this weekend. I'm bringing the love of my life to meet my dearest friends. And for my dearest friends, a pound of espresso coffee beans. See ya soon."

After a few bleeps the line went dead. Gilly stared incredulously into the silence while Anna regarded the receiver sternly. After a punctuated silence, both wandered away. Throughout the day, any time either passed the living room, they surveyed the gadget with wary, respectful glances.

A telephone that answers itself. What next? Prior to their demise, Gilly had come to see television as an irritating intrusion, although she admitted that "The Ed Sullivan Show" was entertaining. If they could invent television and talking telephones, God only knew what else was going on out there.

The remainder of the day passed uneventfully, and ultimately Anna went outside to rid herself of further thoughts on modern technology. Gilly however, spent much of the day in thought. Abundant change was once again perched on the doorstep. Only this time Gilly sensed that it was not the same as in the past. Nothing obtrusive had been done to the house. Moreover, Gilly had the feeling that whoever was about to arrive would prove different from the earlier visitors who were so full of dark emotions. In fact, the times Gilly had entered the house after the soon-to-be occupants had been inside, the place seemed none the worse for them.

Anna disengaged herself from the flowers and drifted into the house. "I came inside because I feel we are about to have company," she said matter-of-factly. She stood for a moment, head to the side, staring again at the telephone. A red signal light blinked rapidly. With a slight shrug of her shoulders she glanced to the window where Gilly remained perfectly still. "In fact, I'm sure of it."

"Uhmm," Gilly replied, still looking out toward the road. "I'd say you are absolutely right, Anna. If you'll step over here a little you'll see what I mean."

Anna moved closer. Dusk had fallen in earnest; bright sunlight was fading to a soft purplish glow. A car was just turning from the road onto the long drive leading to the house.

The car was blue and oddly shaped, having a sharp slant in front and an oversized backseat area with big windows. It carried two passengers. There was nothing shy about the way the car sped up the drive, bouncing and jiggling around deep potholes. The car came to a sharp stop at the gate leading to the walkway. The setting sun created an orange halo that appeared attached to the car's rear bumper.

Doors flung wide as two women stepped from the car. One stood beside the opened driver's side door and stared at the house, while the other exploded from the passenger side and began talking and waving her arms at once. "C'mon," she yelped, grabbing her companion by the arm. Together they half walked, half stumbled up the pathway to the door.

From an upstairs window the spirits peered down at the unsuspecting newcomers. "There's a bit of Cherokee in that taller one," Gilly said. "I can tell by the cheekbones and those broad white teeth. She reminds me of a Wac I knew at Camp Pershing."

Anna looked at Gilly slightly askance but decided to ignore the remark. She was Gilly's only lover, and Gilly hers. Whatever it was that had created the two of them especially for each other she couldn't fathom, but was, she could now say with surety, eternally grateful.

"Yes. And the other one puts me in mind of little Margaret O'Brien, only older of course, and heavier," Anna added. "I wonder what ever happened to Margaret O'Brien? She was so cute in *Little Women.*"

There was hardly time to discuss the matter of Margaret O'Brien or her destiny, for just as Anna spoke the two women pulled open the door and hurtled into the living room. "Oh, god," Gilly heard one of them gasp. "Oh my god. It's perfect."

With only the quickest glance at each other, the spirits swirled down the stairs in unison. On entering the living room, and with mild surprise, they found the two women standing very close together in the middle of the floor, arms around each other. "I'm just so happy," said the one who looked like Margaret O'Brien, and with that she nestled her head in the crook of the other's shoulder before planting a loud, wet kiss there.

"I suppose they're sisters," Anna said softly. "Isn't that sweet. No wonder we didn't notice anything heavy or unpleasant about the place after they had been here. No fat husband clomping about."

"Perhaps," Gilly answered, but her eyes remained

glued to the spot where lips touched neck. Fascinated, she stared at the lovely pink glow that spread through the skin and flesh of the kissee. "Perhaps not."

There was only the briefest look between Gilly and Anna as the silence was suddenly broken by a loud yelp.

"Look. There's a message on the machine," one of them said and broke away.

"So what," laughed the other.

"We aren't ruled by appointment books and answering machines anymore. We're free!"

"Not so," the tall one called out. "What if it's my broker. That stock split I've been waiting for might have been announced today. I've got to find out . . ." She loped toward the telephone. She wore a soft baggy sweater and even baggier shorts. From the shorts to a pair of canvas hiking boots were long muscular legs that flexed pleasantly when she walked. She pressed a button and the message — the source of so much earlier consternation for Gilly and Anna — was replayed. "Hah!" she hooted when the message finished. "That was no news flash. Marsha was in love with someone last week, and, if I remember right, the week before that. Surely no one in her right mind would be caught dead without her own espresso in a place like this."

"She's a pistol," Margaret O'Brien said. "We've now met at least three new loves in as many months. Where does she find the stamina? It sounds perfectly gruesome to me, all that wining and dining. A new woman to get to know every few days. I'd get confused and end up calling the wrong name at the right moment. But, I must say, I sort of envy her all of that great sex."

The taller woman stiffened slightly and reddened. "Well, whatever. They'll be here soon enough, oozing hormones. And we've got so much to do to get ready."

"Right you are, my sweet Ellie." She flung an arm around her companion's waist. "Try to remember your promise. This is supposed to be fun. We've barely set foot in the place, and I want to see every nook and cranny before we so much as unpack a towel. And," she said, tracing a finger playfully along Ellie's cheek, "I'd like a little romancing. For instance, you could waltz me around here in this wonderful moonlight."

"You know I can't dance, Tessa. Besides, there's no music."

"Fuddy-duddy. I'm taking you under my tutelage, my dear Ellie. And, believe me, when I'm done, you'll be a new woman," not Margaret O'Brien at all but someone named Tessa replied. She tossed her pony tail, and one of her large, silver ear hoops danced in the last of the light. "I guess, after all these years, a bit of the magic might have worn thin in our relationship, m'dear." She twisted a loose tendril of hair between her fingers and smiled up at Ellie Holiday, her lover these past six years, and playfully batted her eyes. "But, I'm hoping a little country air will change all that."

"I'd say it'll take more than country air to revive the kind of earth shattering, cosmic, see-god-and-raise-you-one sex we had in the beginning. It's just not realistic. We've gotten too accustomed to one another. I'm just too predictable —"

"Au contraire. You remain one of the most unpredictable women I've ever known. Take our winding up here as only one example. I thought that for the rest of your days you would remain joined at the hip to margin calls, pork bellies, and the Dow-Jones average. Yet mere months later, here we are in a truly beautiful and, might I add, romantic setting, and there's not a *Wall Street Journal* in sight."

"Go figure," Ellie grinned, her coppery face a billboard of pleasure in self and circumstance. "And if living in the country and running a bed-and-breakfast contains within it the germ of a rekindled sex life, then we're going to be very busy little bees indeed."

"To be sure!" Tessa peeled off her backpack and tossed it into a corner. "Now, weren't you going to waltz me around here, or something?"

Gilly and Anna shimmered close to each other and watched the departing figures most intently. "Well," murmured Gilly, half to herself. "Well," echoed Anna.

The house was bathed in silver from a newly risen moon. The shiny new paint on the windows caught the light and turned it an iridescent blue. Anna moved to follow the pair, all but materializing in the deep ochre of anticipation. Gilly allowed herself a short bask in the beautiful mix of colors.

Anna twirled around. "Gilly. Do you suppose —" Without waiting for Anna to finish Gilly sang out, "I don't know, Anna. I thought we were the only ones to feel, um, well, to feel that way."

"So did I. But they were, you know. Well, you saw it, too. They kissed each other."

By midmorning the following day, the house, brightly lit by a cloudless day, remained silent. After a tour of the house and grounds the women had finished off the wine and fallen deeply asleep on sleeping bags they had spread in the parlor.

Gilly had agreed with Anna to avoid any nocturnal activity outside the house, and they had spent the entire night watching the sleeping pair. Tessa and Ellie had been unaware of their observers. They slept curled around each other; the night was an assortment of twining and releasing legs and arms and hands.

As the sun inched higher, muffled sounds filled the downstairs of the house. Gilly and Anna, who had remained at their posts, were unaccustomed to such noise but did not find the disturbance unpleasant. To the contrary, each wanted the new day to begin. There was much they wanted to know, to observe, and to find out. Whatever the joys, discoveries, and understanding the afterlife might have had to offer this day would pale in comparison to the adventure of spying on Ellie and Tessa.

At last the young women got up, and soon the

aroma of coffee permeated the house. "My, my, that smells good," Anna sighed. "I'd forgotten how wonderful morning smells when coffee is perking."

"Oh, lordy. Me, too. I'd even forgotten how much I loved the stuff."

"Way too much for your own good," Anna replied smartly.

"Be that as it may, wouldn't a cup of that taste wonderful? I bet we could, too. Have a cup of coffee, I mean. We could just suck up the essence — like the daffodils and any number of other essences we've sampled."

In the kitchen Ellie slurped her coffee noisily while Tessa blew across the top of hers to cool it. "I can't believe how lucky we are," Tessa said after her first gulp. "Can you believe it? All that wonderful furniture and those forties memorabilia just sitting out there in the barn. We won't have to buy a thing for the house. It's all there. Man, what a day."

Ellie grinned broadly, exposing her large white teeth. "It's fabulous! Imagine, all that great period stuff. That would cost a fortune these days — if you could even find things like that in the stores. Out on Melrose Avenue we'd have to hock everything to furnish our little home and business like that. We'll have to go into town and buy massive numbers of plants. Wouldn't a huge hanging fern look great over the wicker table and rocker? Let's start bringing it all in as soon as we finish our coffee."

After throwing on jeans, tank tops, and what Anna considered very bulky sneakers, Ellie and Tessa barged out the back door amid good-natured whooping and yelling.

* * * * *

"C'mon, Anna," Gilly roared, feeling extremely good natured and expansive. "We're going to enjoy a cup of joe." The day seemed adventuresome and filled with promise. "Nothing like a stiff cup of java to add starch to the spirit."

In the kitchen Gilly and Anna hovered over the coffee maker. Nonplussed due to lengthy experience in such matters, they drew the essence of the coffee inward, savoring the strong, bitter flavor and feeling the warmth as it permeated their spirit selves. "My god," Gilly half swooned. "My god, this is good."

"You know it! But look, Gilly. The level of coffee in the pot is decreasing. In fact, it's almost all gone."

"Well, how do you like that? Greedy, weren't we."

Gilly suddenly felt as if she were made of electricity. She whirled and buzzed and by her estimation so did Anna, who resembled a Fourth of July sparkler as she moved into the living room. Not having had coffee for several decades, the effect was stunning. Gilly suddenly regretted her overindulgence as she now dreaded the effort it would take to remove herself from the ceiling.

The door flew open and Ellie struggled in, backside first. She held one end of a long sofa; Tessa maneuvered the other. Carefully they set the sofa on the long wall facing the windows, then flopped down on it panting.

Tessa ran her hand lovingly over the velvet cushions, the burnished wood, and the cane. "What a find," she exclaimed. "I had a friend once who spent months prowling secondhand stores all over Los

Angeles County looking for one of these. And there's a chair to match, and all those other wonderful things. The barn is just stuffed full — spool beds, wicker. Did you see that ornate parrot cage?"

"Quite the assortment out there. All those instruments and what appears to be box upon box of music. Very interesting."

"Very. And you know what else? I have a feeling all this belonged to a couple of women. Did you notice the clothes, and those boxes labeled with either 'Gilly' or 'Anna?' "

"Maybe 'Gilly' was a man?"

"Doubt it. Not unless he was a drag queen. Did you check out those ball gowns and slinky dresses?"

"No. I haven't seen those yet. It'll take days to go through all that's out there." Ellie paused for just a sliver, "But I didn't feel anything male about any of it."

"Uhmmm," said Tessa.

"Uhmmm," said Ellie.

Later in the afternoon, Ellie and Tessa unpacked in an upstairs bedroom. Several cartons sat on the bed, their contents fully or partially strewn over the coverlet. Tessa stood at the foot of the bed looking down, a glow of perspiration on the bridge of her nose and across her hairline. Ellie sat, legs akimbo, in a wildly flowered wing chair. "Well, what do you know," she said softly.

Tessa directed a puff of breath at her bangs and tentatively touched one of the many objects lying on the bed's surface. She picked up a faded record album and wiped a layer of dust from the jacket with the sleeve of her shirt. "Boogie-Woogie Babes," she read from the cover, although it sounded more a question. "And just look at the songs. 'A-Train,' 'Don't Sit Under the Apple Tree,' even 'Chattanooga Choo Choo.' Wow, what a great forties collection. Who the hell were the Musi-Gals, I wonder?"

Gilly and Anna, watching through an open doorway, stirred uncomfortably. True, the music had been recorded over fifty years ago during that concert in the Philippines, but still it was difficult. Anna said forcefully, "It's us!" But of course no one heard her. But, that was okay. She figured that, left to their investigation, the two young women would soon enough discover just who, indeed, were the Musi-Gals, at least the two most featured members. Tessa meanwhile had walked to the bed and was examining a spangled cummerbund. "They were entertainers," she announced, wrapping the faded cummerbund around her waist.

"I'll tell you more than that," Ellie smiled broadly, setting up her coup. "Here's a picture of them. It's hard to see through the grime and it's awfully faded, but I think we've just met the previous owners of the Blue Heron Bed and Breakfast for discriminating lesbians." She handed the album cover to Tessa. "Look for yourself."

Tessa stared at the yellowed photograph. Sure enough, it was a picture of an all-girl band, probably from the forties. *The Musi-Gals,* the lettering on the drums and music stands announced. Two women stood in front of the group, grinning broadly and holding hands. The one with the saxophone strapped around her neck was tall with a short bob, the other wore her hair in a page boy and looked as if she summered in Côte d'Azur. The picture conveyed an unmistakable esprit de corps, especially between the two women standing out front.

"Well, what do you know," Ellie said, repeating Tessa's comment of a few moments earlier. "See if you can read the little bitty print at the bottom."

"Says here the two in front are, respectively, a Gillian Pettibone and an Anna something. McGath or McGraw. I can't quite make it out."

Anna, uncharacteristically, did not take offense, but Gilly, who was having a roaring good time, yelped, "McGraw. Anna McGraw. She could belt out a tune to put Fitzgerald to shame. And talk about your scat —" She nudged Anna in the place where her ribs might have been. "That girl was the hottest thing on the USO circuit. Not to mention mine!"

"Honestly, Gilly," Anna whispered, though she had turned a pleasant pale rose. "You old scoundrel. Had it not been for you I might have lived a circumspect life, say as an Episcopal minister's wife."

"Ummm. Now wouldn't that have been a waste."

"Exactly. You have my eternal thanks," Anna winked and linked her arm through Gilly's. The fun was only beginning, and the party promised to last into the night.

Some while later the new arrivals, each balancing a freshly made cappuccino, stared at the faded mementos they had brought downstairs and spread over the coffee table. Tessa took a sip of the steaming coffee and stared thoughtfully at the photos. "Know what?"

"No. What?"

Tessa continued flipping the brittle pages of the scrapbook without looking up. "I have a funny feeling about something."

Ellie looked up. "About what, honey?"

Tessa squirmed around so that she looked out the long, high windows toward the Sound. "Promise you won't laugh or think I'm a nut case?"

"I promise," Ellie laughed. "What's this all about?"

"What if I told you that I get the feeling these two women from the past are, well — are still around here, ah, somehow."

Ellie whooped with laughter. "Oh, Tessa. You are the most wonderful, wacky —"

"El, I'm serious."

"Oh, baby. That's ridiculous. There's no such thing as ghosts." Again Ellie laughed. She moved next to Tessa on the sofa and pulled her closer.

Tessa tensed. "You said you wouldn't laugh. Damn it, El. You're just so linear."

Ellie let her arms fall back to the sofa. "Okay, okay. I'm sorry. I wasn't making fun of you. It's just that sometimes you're so, I don't know, so whimsical. Well," she brought her palms down on her knees, "what makes you think there are ghosts in our wonderful new place?"

"Just a feeling," Tessa answered, a slight edge in her tone.

"You mean you haven't seen any ectoplasm, emanations, floating shrouds, anything like that?"

"No, of course not. Now you're being silly."

"Well, I'm relieved to hear it." Ellie stretched her legs and crossed them, lacing her hands behind her neck. "Nothing could be worse than a couple of old spooks drifting from room to room, scaring the wits out of our lavishly accommodated guests. If that sort of news got around, we'd be closed inside of a month."

Tessa took another sip of her coffee, staring for a long time into the rich, creamy liquid. She loved Ellie with all her heart, but everything in her yearned for another plane of understanding between them. If El couldn't see it, touch it, or devise a mathematical equation to explain it, for her it didn't exist. Once Tessa had wanted them to attend a new group of several women who met once a week to explore women's spirituality. When Tessa mentioned the group, Ellie had snorted derisively and announced she wouldn't be caught dead holding hands in a circle with a bunch of fruitcakes who probably spelled *women* w-i-m-m-i-n.

Deciding the age-old question between discretion and valor, Tessa set her coffee cup on the table. To say more at that point could provoke an argument, and the day was too full of promise to spoil. Anyway, the feeling about not being alone was vague. She couldn't pin it down to a specific event. She couldn't explain it, especially to someone whose negative response was a foregone conclusion.

"I think I'll run upstairs and start putting linens on the bed in the back bedroom. Marsha and number four will be here tonight, and we've got lots to do before then." Ellie stood and stretched. "That is, if we're all done talking about ghosts. Honestly," she ruffled Tessa's hair, "you have the wildest imagination. As far as I'm concerned, there's no such thing as ghosts. When you're dead, you're dead. That's it. The end. Finis. I can't fathom the concept of eternity, let alone think what I'd do with all that extra time. Trust me, darlin'. We are the sole inhabitants of this wonderful, endlessly bucolic setting. Now, I've got to get busy."

Tessa absently picked up a strand of twine that lay on the coffee table and began winding it into a ball. "Oh, okay. You're probably right. But in a weird way, I wish you weren't. I'd kind of like it if we had a bonafide ghost."

"Oh right. And instead of offering our guests wine and cheese on the sunporch at four every afternoon, we could host a seance." Ellie grinned and jammed her hands into the pockets of her shorts. "C'mon. Give me a hand upstairs. It'll go faster if we both work at getting the room ready."

Tessa rose, dropping the ball of twine she had rolled onto the table, and followed Ellie up the stairs. Maybe El was right. Being out in the country, so isolated and with no one to talk to, played tricks on the imagination.

Twelve

Tessa dipped a plate into the sudsy water and scrubbed. Ellie, her head cocked toward the living room, polished another dinner plate to a high sheen. "Wash slower," she commanded. "They're still at it."

"Maybe it was the oysters."

"Hmmmp. They couldn't keep their hands off one another long enough to eat any of them." Ellie grinned and leaned closer toward the door, peeking at the two women kissing and groaning and sweating on the pretty cane-backed sofa. She and Tessa had gone all out on a Northwest banquet for Marsha and her new friend, Lynn. They had started with fresh oysters on the half shell, followed by chilled cracked crab. Whole lobster with drawn butter and chocolate torte with homemade raspberry sauce rounded out the menu. But neither Marsha nor Lynn had seemed much interested.

Instead of eating, they had cast half-lidded looks of longing across their plates and punctuated lapses in conversation with long, wet kisses. The oysters had proven the perfect foil for many double entendres, and just watching the lovers turn up the shell and slide the wet, slick meat into the mouth of the other was enough to make even Tessa blush.

Ellie dried another plate and set it carefully in the drainer. She raised her eyebrows in an archly disapproving parody. "Not that it matters, but did you notice how difficult it was to have an intelligent conversation about the role of the PLO in the Middle East crisis?"

Tessa whooped with laughter, sloshing dishwater and almost dropping a china cup. "Uh huh," she finally managed, "and I noted a certain lack of interest in the current failure of local government to deal with the homeless problem." Tessa drew her arm across her face, wiping away dishwater and tears of laughter.

"They'll get over it. After all, they've only been together for forty-eight hours or so. What did we expect?"

"Oh, I know they will. And sooner or later, we'll have Marsha back, acerbic wit and all. Then we can have an entertaining dinner conversation again. Meanwhile, let's finish these dishes and sneak upstairs. We'll never be missed and, frankly, the evening has proven stimulating, if you know what I mean."

"I do indeed. In fact, they remind me of us in our first bloom of love. God, remember that time —"

"Let's not talk about it, my sweet, let's just, as the current expression goes, do it."

Later, as Tessa and Ellie lay in each other's arms, Tessa said in a voice just barely back in her control, "God, I wish I still smoked. I miss the after-sex cigarette most of all. I don't know what to do with my hands." She grinned at Ellie and turned to face her. "Of course, having you so close gives me a thought or two in that direction."

"You're incorrigible," Ellie laughed and kissed Tessa tenderly on the mouth, a mouth still swollen and slightly red. "But, I love it."

"I believe we should alert the media," Tessa nibbled at Ellie's ear. "There's a story of major importance."

"Oh? And what might that be?"

"Flash: Dyke couple discover sex is alive and well in lesbian relationships well after the three-year mark."

"I admit, it was rather amazing. I'll let you have CNN if you'll let me do 'Oprah.' "

"Amazing is hardly the word. You were faaantastic. I've never, well, you know, so many times."

Ellie blushed, once again feeling the rush of heat, the stab of passion in her groin. "What's with us, anyway?" she asked, her voice becoming husky. "I feel like an eighteen-year-old." Ellie slid her hand along Tessa's glistening, smooth belly, stopping just at the line of soft hair. She let her fingers linger there.

"No, not yet." Tessa placed her hand over Ellie's stopping the delicate, delicious roaming. "One more second, and I'll be a goner. I want to make love to you." She drew Ellie's hand to her mouth, kissed it, and placed it over her breast as she rolled over onto Ellie, her tongue tracing the skin along Ellie's neck.

With a groan Ellie scooted lower, so that her mouth and Tessa's were at the same level. She left a butterfly kiss there, then lay back on the pillow, consumed by Tessa's mouth and tongue and hands and arms until she felt she no longer knew where her body left off and Tessa's began. She knew that Tessa's head was between her legs and that the sensations radiating through her body, even her soul, carried her outside her body, the bed, the room, into a limitless space of exploding light and color. At the moment she could bear it no longer she cried out, shuddered and, jamming her fist into her mouth to muffle the scream of her pleasure, floated reluctantly back to earth.

Gilly and Anna, who had arranged themselves in the downstairs parlor after everyone had gone to bed, sat motionless on the sofa. Anna, glowing bright pink, giggled and raised a hand to her mouth. She glanced at Gilly but did not speak. She made a great show of clearing her throat and attempted to say something but collapsed into giggles again.

"Well," Gilly said after some while. "Well, well." But she couldn't seem to go on. She closed her mouth and sat next to Anna, glowing the same neon pink.

They had hovered near the table at dinner, fascinated by the antics of the two guests. "Oysters, my foot!" Gilly had exclaimed later as Ellie and Tessa did the dishes. "That was quite the performance."

"Ummm. Puts me in mind of a couple of other evenings of my acquaintance." Anna looked at Gilly, smiling her slow, dreamy smile.

"So it does," Gilly replied, returning the smile in the identical manner. "But that was back when we were still in bodies. Now, of course, we can surpass even the passion of first love. Right, my love?"

"Never would I have dreamed that bodies could get in the way where sex is concerned, but these last few decades have convinced me otherwise." Anna cast Gilly a look that bordered upon a leer. "After all, the entire point is the yearning to merge with your lover. If they only knew —"

"The first time you and me — wait, what was the expression they used? — got it on?"

"Uggg!"

"The first time we made love, I thought I saw colors. But until you've experienced the ultimate physical sensation in the very fiber of your spirit, the rest was like an old Bogart and Bacall move — interesting, but in black and white."

Anna grinned. "Very apropos, Miss Pettibone. And to put a finer point on it, there are no words to describe the sensation of feeling the exquisite nature of that little bud between one's legs magnified by the sum of one's entire energy. And to think, scientists consider the splitting of the atom a big deal."

"Yep."

"Don't suppose our lovemaking had anything to do with it?"

"Oh, I'm sure we had a hand in the festivities since our activities influence the people around us. And what a nice thing for us to do. They seemed so pleased with themselves, didn't they?"

Gilly and Anna had hovered around the living room during dinner, fascinated by the newcomers and the unbelievable circumstance of having not one, but two pairs of women loving each other under their roof at the same time. Seeing the two young women so openly intimate with one another and hearing the ragged breath and the gasps had inspired the spirits.

In their spirit form, beds, floors, bathtubs and showers, sandy beaches and, in extreme circumstances, even the backseats of cars were unnecessary. Gilly and Anna merely floated closer to each other, and the sexual power streaked and arced between them like electricity from a high-voltage line. The closer they got to each other, the more acute the sensation from the warm tender spot at the center of passion. The sensation spread out along their spirit selves, filling in every shadow molecule of what had once described their worldly bodies, so that even molecules of hair, toe nail, or wisdom tooth became clitoral, full and red and throbbing with passion.

In the final ecstasy, Gilly and Anna were transported together to a world where all sound was present in silence, where all color glowed and shimmered beyond color, and where release set the spheres of the Milky Way to music, vibrating like the tines of a fine tuning fork.

When it was over, Gilly looked at Anna and said, "When we were alive I used to fear I'd die from the intensity of our loving. Sometime, just before the moment, I'd think to myself, 'Well, old girl, this time it is really over. No human body can withstand such pleasure.' And you know what?"

"I haven't the faintest."

"I couldn't have. Not the way it really can be now. No one could."

"I know," Anna replied. "But isn't it a shame? It's what everyone wants when she loves someone. To feel what her lover feels, to really be inside the other. Too bad we have to wait until we're dead to get it right." Anna giggled again, "I feel so wonderful. Let's do that again, shall we?"

"Why not. The other blessing of the hereafter is that we never need rest."

The following morning dawned rainy and gray, the sun a mere hint of light on the eastern horizon. It was creeping on toward ten A.M. before any of the sleepers disentangled themselves from each other and the downy comforters. Tessa slid out of bed before any of the others and padded softly downstairs, her robe pulled tightly around her to ward off the chill.

She made a pot of coffee, and as the delicious aroma filled the kitchen, she sat quietly and looked around the room. When the coffee was ready she poured herself a cup and went into the living room. She was glad that the others were still sleeping. She needed time alone to sort her feelings. Last night had been wonderful. She and Ellie hadn't made that kind of love in years, maybe ever.

Yet, there was something unusual about their sexual energy, something Tessa couldn't quite name. In a strange way, it seemed as if the sea of sensual bliss had come not only from the two of them, but from the walls, the ceiling, the very air itself. It was spooky, but not in a scary way, just odd and difficult to explain. Once she and Ellie had watched a movie of two women making love. They had been in a group of ten or so other lesbians who had rented the movie as a lark. Tessa had been fully ready to hate the movie, sure the women were mere actors going through the motions and faking pleasure, an experience she likened to consuming dry toast. But it was no porno film. She had watched, absorbed and slightly titillated, as two women who were obviously in love with each other, made wonderful love. They were not only passionate with faces flushed and voices husky, they were by turns tender and forceful and at all times aware of each other's needs and pleasures. The lovemaking continued well past sexual release. The women nuzzled, cuddled, and laughed softly for a long and intimate postlude.

In a way, her experience last night was ever so slightly similar to the night they had watched the movie. But it was different. Just how different, or why, Tessa couldn't say. She sat on the sofa and propped her feet on the coffee table, staring out the window at the misting rain. It was late fall, and the rainy weather would last for months. The sun might make another appearance or two, but soon it would disappear into the gray, thick clouds of the Northwest winter. Tessa sighed and swallowed the last sip of her coffee. "Well," she mouthed as she set down her cup, "whatever the magic was last night, I just hope it lasts."

Marsha plodded down the stairs, looking jumbled and half asleep. "Morning," she mumbled and headed for the kitchen and the coffee pot. Marsha's tall frame was clad in a bedsheet hastily wrapped around her against the cold, and her short blond hair spiked out from her head in wild confusion. She looked grumpy, but since Tessa had never seen her this early in the day, she thought it might just be her usual awaking behavior. Some people did mornings better than others.

"Grab your coffee and join me," Tessa called. "I'll set a fire in the fireplace. I've hardly had a chance to talk with you since you arrived." Tessa said this last with a teasing lilt in her voice. She expected a witty comeback, or at least a laugh, but was greeted with silence from the kitchen.

A few moments later Marsha lumbered into the room and plopped onto the sofa, expelling a long sigh. Tessa, who knelt before the hearth, lit a match to the kindling and turned to face her friend. She grinned at Marsha. "I see we aren't the morning type. That's okay. Just drink your coffee. We can talk after you're fully human again."

Marsha gulped her coffee and made a low noise in her throat. "No," she said, her voice cracking, "I need to talk now. I'm a mess."

"What? After the show you and Lynn put on last

night? How could anyone be a mess after that much affection?"

"Oh, Tessa. My life is over!"

Tessa leaned forward, crossing her arms around her knees, all traces of her intent to chide erased by concern. "What on earth —"

Looking as if she would burst into tears, Marsha hugged herself tightly and rocked back and forth. "Damn it, Tessa. This time I thought it was for real. You know, *the BIG ONE.* I guess I was wrong again."

"But I thought you two just met. I mean, how do you know whether or not Lynn is Mizz Right? After all, these things take time. Relationships are developed, not put in a microwave oven and nuked on high for three minutes. What happened?"

"It's a long story, I guess."

"That's okay. I have all day. Tell me all about it. You met her at the Double Barrel, right? Start from there."

Marsha dabbed at her eyes and looked at Tessa as if trying to decide whether to spread out the whole, sorrowing tale. Then she shrugged and pulled the bedsheet tightly around her. The fire had taken the moist chill from the room, which now glowed cozily in the flickering light.

Marsha told Tessa about the night she and Lynn had met. She had gone to the Double Barrel alone, hoping to find a tableful of friends to hang out with for the evening. The place was jammed when she got there, and at first she didn't see anyone she knew. She was about to turn and leave when she heard her name called across the noise of the band and the general clatter of a boisterous crowd. Up near the tiny dance floor a hand waved energetically in the air. Marsha pushed her way through couples returning from the dance floor between numbers and spied Karen and Maggie, two women she had recently met at an abortion rights rally. One taught at the university and the other was in TV, or something. She made her way toward them.

The crowd bumped and jostled her as she made her way forward. The band, the big draw for the bar, began a new number. That the bar and the band were so spectacularly popular was an anachronism of modern urban life. The bar was located in a seedier section of Pioneer Square so that winos and dykes and street people and drag queens competed for the stools at the long wooden bar along the front. The band, all women save for the tuba player, boasted not one but two accordionists and a drummer. The music ranged from two-steps to waltzes, and the crowd of dancers who came regularly couldn't have been happier. The band had just struck up the first polka of the evening, and dancers rushed to the floor so as not to miss a beat of "Beer Barrel Polka."

Marsha arrived at the crowded table and took a chair that was hastily pulled from nearby. She smiled and tried to catch the names of several women she had not met before. Her eye fell on a small, round-faced woman with huge brown eyes and a short spiked haircut. She couldn't catch her name over the din of the music but was instantly sorry her chair was on the opposite side of the table.

She ordered a beer and danced a two-step with one of her friends. The evening progressed as evenings did at the Double Barrel, and throughout she was most aware of the small, dark-haired woman opposite her. Was it her imagination? It appeared that each time she looked casually around the room secretly trying to catch a glimpse of the woman across the table, the woman quickly looked away.

Marsha asked the woman to dance the very next time the band played a slow number. They folded into each other's arms and against each other's body as if they had been molded with this particular activity in mind. When the song ended, neither fully let go of the other, and Marsha's heart began to race. She pulled the petite woman, whose name she had learned was Lynn, into her arms and they swayed, hardly moving, to "Tennessee Waltz." At the end of the dance they returned to their seats at opposite ends of the huge table, and the looks that darted between them could have scorched the checkered tablecloth.

They had gone home together to Marsha's houseboat on Lake Union, and they had not reappeared until early Monday morning. The next week was crammed with yearning, passion-filled phone calls, take-out dinner every evening, and lovemaking until the sun rose pink and glistening over the lake.

Now, however, Marsha sat wiping away a tear in Tessa's living room as the rain pelted the house and Lynn slept upstairs. "So that's about it. Until this morning, that is." A fresh round of tears sprung to her eyes.

"What happened this morning that was so awful?"

Marsha was about to answer when both women looked up at the sound of someone else on the stairs. Tessa hoped it wasn't Lynn. Marsha might never tell what had gone so suddenly and terribly wrong.

Ellie poked her head into the room and yawned.

"Good god!" she said when she finished the yawn and a satisfying stretch. "It must be noon. Why didn't someone wake me?" Ellie yawned again and trudged toward the kitchen for coffee. "There're a zillion things to do today, and I wanted an early start," she called over her shoulder. "Let me get my coffee and we'll plan a day full of pleasant pastoral pastimes." Ellie giggled and said half to herself, "Ha, ha, I made an alliteration — and before coffee."

"She's in a fine mood," Marsha said. "I've never seen her so active this early in the day."

Tessa started to ask how Marsha knew Ellie's early morning habits, then remembered they had roomed together for a semester in college. "She had a good night," Tessa said and smiled wickedly. "One of the best, if I do say so. But go on Marsha, tell me what is so awfully wrong between you two."

Marsha shifted in her seat. "Well, on the ferry crossing yesterday coming here to see you and Ellie, I asked her to make a commitment. I wanted us to live together on the houseboat. Hell, I even said I'd get a dog. What dyke relationship is complete without a dog? And, I'm allergic to dogs."

"I think you're allergic to patience. But be that as it may, what was her answer?"

"I think you know. She's not ready to make a commitment to anyone yet. She doesn't want to settle down."

"What is she? A baby dyke?"

"Heavens no. Do you take me for a complete fool? She's thirty-four. Ah, but here is the fly in the ointment. She only came out a few months ago. Says she is happy as a pig in a waller and can't think what took her so long. But that's not the worst of it."

"Let me guess. She has a husband and seventeen little kids and doesn't think she can leave them. Right?"

"Wrong. That would be easy. We'd just sneak around till she got over it. Oh, no. It's much worse than that. We didn't really talk about this part until after we woke up early this morning and made love. When we finished, we were smoking a cigarette and she told me the other reason she won't live openly with me or anyone. She's in the closet! Can you imagine? I didn't think anyone was in the closet anymore except maybe movie stars and a few married guys who like to have anonymous sex in the park. Whew! It blew me away."

"Well, gee," Tessa fumbled for words to console her friend. "It isn't like she doesn't care for you. She obviously does. Can't you just take your time, let her have more space to work through this closet thing? She'll probably get over her fear of coming out. After all, she's new to all this."

"I doubt it. Not only is she very close to her family — very Old World Italian by the way, all of whom live in a ten-mile radius of one another — it's her career, too. She says she would lose all hope of promotion and maybe even her job if she came out."

"What does she do for a living that is so warped and narrow?"

"She's a cop. Not just a cop, but a homicide detective moving up the rank and file toward promotion to captain. How do you like them apples, eh?"

"So I don't see the big deal, at least not yet. She doesn't want to settle down anyway. Why don't you just go on enjoying each other's company for a while and let the rest of it wait. And if you think your heart is too involved, just take a step back emotionally and save some of the careening romance for the next one."

"But there won't *be* a next one. Don't you see? She's the *one*. Oh, I'm just miserable. What should I do? I could maybe pull off the playing time for a while, but she says she will never be seen with me on the streets or hold hands in a movie or — oh, god. I'm really in love with her. I just hate to think about living that way — always afraid, always shrinking from whatever or whomever may be lurking around the next corner. I know I look dykey," Marsha ran her hand through her short blond hair, "But I like it. It took me years to perfect my look. I'm proud of being a lesbian."

"I know you are. So am I. And very lucky I don't feel I have to hide. I think you need to give her some more time. Just out of curiosity, where did you plan to get together? Looks like movies and the dyke coffee house are out. But I guess there's always Motel 6." Tessa attempted to smile, but the sour look on Marsha's face made her attempt vanish into the air.

"Well, she thought your place would be a really neat idea. We could meet out here on weekends. Oh, hell —"

Ellie entered the room blowing across her coffee and taking a seat opposite, near the fireplace. "So, my dears, what interesting rural endeavors shall we plan for today? I've got a million ideas. First of all, there are lots of apples out in the orchard ready for picking. Maybe we could make pies later. Or —"

"Ellie," Tessa said softly. "Let's wait a while to make any plans. Marsha isn't feeling so well this morning."

"It was probably the oysters," Ellie said, grinning evilly at Marsha. She stopped when she saw how distraught her friend looked. "Marsha? What's the matter?"

Tessa filled Ellie in on the conversation. At the same time, she moved closer to Marsha on the couch and put her arm around her shoulders. Ellie cleared her throat and stared into her coffee cup. After a moment she spoke. "Aw, Marsha, honey, I know you must hurt. But Tessa's right. Give her some time. You're rushing things. Big time."

Just then Lynn appeared in the doorway. She looked fresh as the new day, her eyes bright, her hair still damp from the shower. "Hi, everybody." Though she had directed the greeting to everyone assembled, her eyes went to Marsha and lingered there. "Hey, you," she smiled.

"Hey," Marsha said and rose to refill her coffee cup.

The sun made a cameo appearance, lighting the room, then disappeared again behind walls of clouds marching inland across the Pacific. Ellie smiled at Lynn and told her where to get a cup of coffee and that bagels were on the counter if she wanted one. She cleared her throat and stared at the floor. God, she hoped Marsha could pull herself together quickly out in the kitchen. She hated a scene, especially a lovers' quarrel when both parties were in your own living room.

"I think I will get myself a cup of coffee," Lynn said and rose. "Get anybody anything?"

Both women returned from the kitchen a short time later, Marsha looking sheepish and Lynn smiling and hold on to Marsha's arm. By what magic Marsha had pulled herself out of her funk, Ellie couldn't say, but she was eternally relieved.

They all dressed in warm clothes and went out to pick apples, promising an apple pie bake-off for the afternoon. All went as Ellie had hoped, and the subject of Marsha's gloom never surfaced again the rest of the day.

Toward dark, the house redolent with the smell of several high-crusted, flaky apple pies, Marsha and Lynn said their good-byes. They wanted to take an early ferry back to Seattle. They had muttered something about an appointment, but Ellie suspected they were headed straight for the houseboat and bed.

Ellie and Tessa waved good-bye at the door and then headed for the stairs and bed themselves. It had been a long time since they had spent most of the night awake, and they were bone tired.

"Closet?" Gilly pondered the word and its meaning, her spectral chin in her hand. "So that's where we've been all this time."

"Very apt expression, too, if you ask me. Closets are dark and musty at best and don't let in any light."

"But we made the best of a bad situation, I'd say, given the times we lived in."

"We did indeed. Maybe we kept ourselves hidden away, separate in our own little world. But that world was so full of light — and love."

"Was?" Gilly arched her brows.

"You know what I mean. And speaking of times, seems that in our absence, the times have done a good deal of changing. Those young women all seem so, I don't know, so open about loving each other."

"And there is a bar where they go to dance — with each other? What was it called, the Double Barrel? I wonder what else might be going on out there?"

"Me too!"

"Ummm," said Gilly.

"Ummm," said Anna.

Thirteen

By the reckoning of the weather service, snow would descend on the Northwest by evening, the first storm of the season. Tessa had gone to town to stock up on candles and bottled water in case the power went out or the pipes froze. Ellie sat at the kitchen table, hunched over the books for the Blue Heron Bed and Breakfast. The wind had kicked up considerably over the last hour, and the low, pewter clouds appeared to prove the weather service right. Snow would be falling in short order.

Ellie scowled and scratched through a column of

numbers. She began a new column, carefully copying amounts owed from a stack of unpaid bills and biting her lip in concentration. Beside her, the coffee had grown cold and a jumble of wadded papers littered the floor. *A lot of good my fancy MBA does me with this,* she thought sourly. *I'd have been better off to put my money in high-risk bonds than in this damn bed-and-breakfast..*

Since opening, the bed-and-breakfast had gone the way of many newly conceived small businesses. There were more bills and more start-up costs than income. There had been guests, but not many and not often enough.

Ellie laid down her pen, an expensive, gold-plated gift from her former co-workers. She stretched and looked to see if it had started to snow. She paced the kitchen, then the living room, trying to think what else she and Tessa might do to increase business. It wasn't as if they would lose every cent if the place failed — they had plenty squirreled away — it was that Tessa had wanted it so badly. From the day they had begun to talk about moving to the country and starting a small business, Tessa had been a woman transformed. Ellie knew that Tessa had wanted change for them both, but especially for her. Tessa felt, and rightfully so, that Ellie was far too caught up in making money and having "things" and had let a large and vital part of her go unnourished, but, by god, it was costing her a bundle.

Tessa had been right. She had come to feel more relaxed, more aware, since moving to this beautiful country setting. Back in Seattle, she wouldn't have known a rhododendron from a hubcap. Here, she not only knew what a rhododendron was, she had even taken to calling the ones out by the lane by name! Perhaps it was something in the country air, some alchemy of atmosphere, that caused a slowing, a calming of the frenetic pace she had always accepted as normal.

And then there was her rekindled love life. She and Tessa made love as if they were new lovers—often and with breathless passion. Talk about mystical atmospheres! By what magic potion had that come about? Ellie walked back into the kitchen, determined to balance the books by noon and just as determined to stay the course, whatever the cost.

In a little while she heard Tessa driving up the lane and hurriedly gathered up the debris of her session with the accounts. She scooped bills into a marked folder and gathered the wadded paper into the trash. When she finished, she stood staring at the bare table, searching for her pen. Unable to find it, she looked on the floor under the table and sorted through the papers in the trash. Still no pen. Just then Tessa burst through the back door and whooped. "My god, it's cold. The first snowflakes are coming down. I hope you've got a fire going."

Tessa dropped her bundles on the counter and moved to stand behind Ellie, putting her arms around her. She nuzzled her neck. "What have you been up to, sweetie?"

"Nothing much. Just going over some of the accounts."

"Yeah? Pretty bad, huh?"

"Grim, indeed. But right now I'm searching for my pen. I'd swear I had it right here when I was working on the books. Now it's disappeared. Help me look for it, will you? I'd really hate to lose it."

When a search for the missing pen turned up nothing, Ellie made sandwiches and the two ate while watching the lazy drift of the falling snow from the kitchen window. Ellie had just finished her sandwich and was about to take up the search again when the phone rang. Tessa went to answer, and when she returned to the kitchen she smiled and held up two fingers in a victory symbol. "Guess what," she bubbled, very excited. "We have guests arriving. And guess what else." Tessa drew out the suspense with a dramatic pause. "They're staying for two weeks!"

"Wow, two weeks. We're rich!" Ellie grabbed Tessa and danced her around the kitchen in a little jig. "I'll have to run to the store. We'll need fresh eggs, and I'll make a pan of my yet-to-become-famous blueberry muffins for breakfast. By the way, who are these women coming to stay two whole weeks in an isolated B and B in the middle of winter?"

"Winter won't bother these women. They're from Switzerland, somewhere in the Alps. They're in the U.S. on an extended vacation and said they might even want to stay longer." Tessa spun around and walked back to the kitchen. After a moment, she called, "Hey, I thought you said you'd lost your pen. It's right here on the table."

Ellie walked swiftly into the room, staring at the shiny surface of the round oak table. Sure enough, there her fancy fountain pen lay. How on earth could she not have seen it right there in the open?

Tessa ran upstairs to tidy up and put clean linens in the guest room while Ellie stared at the pen on the table. In her world, things did not simply disappear only to reappear again out of thin air. No indeed. Ellie's world was precise, mathematically so.

And the behavior of the fountain pen was an imprecise intrusion into her ordered existence. Tessa was always talking about her feeling that they did not inhabit the old house alone, and more so the longer they were in residence. Ellie had pooh-poohed her relentlessly. Ellie shook her head at the sight of the shiny gold pen. So much had changed since she had come here — about herself, her beliefs, who knew what else. A short while later she left the kitchen to join Tessa upstairs, but she could not dislodge the mystery of the pen from her mind.

Anna wafted near the long bank of windows in the living room, enjoying the kaleidoscope of geometric shapes in each snowflake. She studiously ignored Gilly, who felt she shouldn't have taken the pen. Anna didn't feel the little caprice was harmful. After all, Ellie hadn't been frightened. Merely puzzled. And for reasons even she couldn't fully fathom, Anna really wanted Tessa and Ellie to know she and Gilly were there. More than that, she wanted to make friends with them. What they talked about, their friends, the lives they seemed to lead, fascinated her, and she had told Gilly as much earlier that morning.

"Me, too," Gilly said emphatically and with great enthusiasm. "What a place the world seems to be now. Nothing like you or I could ever have dreamed. Can you imagine what it must be like to live openly and not fear exposure — or something worse?"

Both spirits contemplated such a life, turning the palest twilight blue of yearning. Gilly remembered their last hours at Camp Pershing, all those years ago, and wondered how different that awful day might have been had they lived in such a world then. And from that watershed event right down to the ordinary, everyday aspects of life, she knew curiosity and even a vague longing. Just the simple act of a group of like-minded friends, chatting away after dinner, talking of their lives and loves, seemed so comforting, so supportive. And that place they all talked about, the Double Barrel. What must it be like to hold your lover close and sway to the music in full view of others?

As though reading her mind, which she was, Anna purred, "Wouldn't it be fun to go to that bar one night. Just imagine, polkas and fox trots and waltzes! We could really cut a rug."

"Oh my, yes. It would be fun," Gilly said smiling. "But of course that's impossible."

"Of course it is," Anna said, turning away and hoping Gilly wouldn't notice the smug, self-satisfied smile that played along her face and spread a deep rose glow of anticipation across the snow-filled yard.

Some evenings later, an exhausted Tessa and Ellie sat in the cozy living room, trying to keep up with the ricocheting conversation and curiosity of four strapping, hearty Swiss women. As usual, Gilly and Anna hovered nearby eavesdropping.

At first, when the group of two had proven, through a miscommunication, to be four, Tessa had whooped with delight, and Ellie had felt her financial troubles begin to vanish. The snow had melted, the pipes had not burst, and due to the unscheduled arrival of another two guests, they had a full house. All eight of them now sat around the flickering fireplace, pleasantly sated with good food and wine.

Earlier they had tromped out to a section of woods behind the house where, for years, a neighbor's goats had trespassed and eaten the bark from a number of trees. The trees had died long years past, but many still stood rooted in the ground. Felling trees, cutting them into lengths, and splitting the logs for the fireplace had long ago become old hat for Tessa and Ellie, but it sounded like enormous fun to the guests. So clad in boots and windbreakers and heavy gloves, they had set eagerly about the tasks of replenishing the firewood.

As they now sat by the fire, exhaustion showed plainly on the face of each hostess, though both smiled and attempted to keep up with the quiet, murmuring conversation. By earlier agreement, they planned a signal whereby either could indicate bedtime and they would gracefully rise and depart for the comfort of flannel sheets and mounds of blankets. Tessa was about to raise her hand in the prearranged signal when one of the guests, an older, bookish woman traveling alone, said into the warm, comfortable air, "You know, I think you may have a ghost in here."

Ellie stopped her arm in mid-air. Her brows shot up, her eyes grew wide.

"Ja?" cried one of the Swiss women.

To Tessa's delight and Ellie's consternation, within a short few excited moments the group created a homemade Ouija board. They printed letters on a piece of cardboard and used a small, wrought iron trivet as the planchette. Someone suggested they light candles.

With great excitement and chattering in broken English, the Swiss women arranged themselves in a circle on the floor, followed by the other guests and Ellie. Tessa returned with candles and joined the group. With fingers placed lightly on the trivet, the seance began.

At first nothing happened. Then without fanfare the planchette began to skitter around the board, lighting on a letter or numeral before skidding away to another. "Who's doing that?" Ellie demanded. When no one confessed, she snorted in derision, but her eyes held a certain mystified, all but incredulous glaze. Feeling ridiculous, she continued holding her fingers on the planchette but announced for the benefit of all assembled that this was silly. There is no such thing as a ghost.

The careening planchette swooped and dipped around the board, stretching the arms and imaginations of the assembled women. Finally, limbs aching from the excessive activity, someone suggested that since it was Tessa and Ellie's house, they alone should touch the planchette. That way, someone else could write down the letters spelled out as the planchette dashed and cavorted over the board. Reluctantly, yet somehow drawn to the peculiar energy that coursed along the board, Ellie joined Tessa in placing her fingers lightly on the planchette.

Now the energy slowed, became less frantic. And to Ellie's astonishment, the planchette moved. Not in little, weak patterns, but in forceful, purposeful moves. Wide-eyed, Ellie looked at Tessa and saw her slightly lopsided smile, the warm satisfaction glowing in her face. "Told you so," she said, her grin widening. "Let's ask the spirit if it has a message for us."

Ellie shaped her mouth around a derisive comment, but stopped the sounds in her throat. She just might be wrong about ghosts, after all. She swallowed hard and nodded. "Okay. What should we ask?" she practically squeaked.

"Let's start by asking who is trying to communicate with us."

Having so said, the planchette began to dance over the board. The planchette skidded to the letter *A,* then did a wild, circular dance in the middle of the board before careening to land on the letter *G.* The color drained from Ellie's face.

"Oh my god," Tessa shrieked. Everyone in the room grew silent and stared at Tessa, who had clapped her hand to her mouth. "Oh my god," she repeated. "It's the women who left all that great stuff here. The ones who lived here for so long. Oh lord. They're still here."

Ellie gulped. "Let's try again. It could just be coincidence." To her half delight, several more attempts produced the exact same result. *G* and *A* were repeatedly spelled out by the little planchette. "Oh my lord," Ellie said softly. "Oh my lord."

Soon after, the energy that moved the planchette seemed to grow weaker, and each attempt to get a response became more and more like trying to start a car with a battery that is rapidly losing juice. The Swiss women who had compiled a list of questions for the Ouija to answer, mostly concerning upcoming love affairs, were disappointed but still animated. The session had left Tessa and Ellie enervated. They had been tired before, but now Tessa felt it would be all she could do to climb the stairs for bed. "I'm beat," she announced. "Maybe we can try again tomorrow night. I'm off to bed. You coming, Ellie?"

"Bed!" a Swiss guest cried. "Nein. There is so much to do here. We go dancing, ja? That place you all go so much, the Double Barrel."

After checking the schedule for the ferryboat across the Sound to Seattle, the Swiss women trooped out, leaving Tessa and Ellie and the other two women to fall exhausted into their respective beds.

With the living room now deserted, Gilly and Anna swirled close together, enjoying the last embers of the fire. "Whew! That was hard." Anna exclaimed. "But what fun!"

Gilly grinned a silly flamingo smile. "Sending that little trivet flying was like trying to direct a feather with your breath. I'm all but used up of essence. But at least we got our initials across. They know about us."

"I hope we can all become friends, don't you? I'm so curious about the world out there. We'll learn a lot from them. I only wish . . ." Anna hesitated, not sure Gilly was ripe for the subject she was about to broach.

"Wish what?" Gilly asked in her most encouraging voice. The evening had been rich with fun. Perhaps Anna had another trick up her sleeve. The one about playing along with the Ouija board game had been a doozy.

Anna thought for a good while before answering.

She had been thinking about something for quite a while, something she wasn't sure how to broach with Gilly. Her plan was outlandish, and there was a chance Gilly would reject the notion out of hand. But the very thought of doing it kept Anna in a state of anticipation and excitement. "I was only going to say, I wish we could go out to that place they all go, the Double Barrel."

"Well, I suppose we could just beam ourselves over the Sound and into Seattle. It's in Pioneer Square somewhere. I'm sure we could find the place. And," she added with a grin, "we certainly wouldn't have to pay a cover charge."

"That's not exactly what I mean, m'dear."

There was a long pause before Gilly exclaimed, her aura deepening with shock, "No. Oh, Anna. Forget it. We couldn't do that?"

"Why not?"

"It just wouldn't be right. Cats, maybe. And herons. But people?"

"Oh, Gilly. Don't be such a fuddy-duddy. Just think of the possibilities."

"I am. I'm thinking about slipping into the bodies of two very alive young women and traipsing about all over god knows where. What if they wake up and we're still in there?"

"I haven't thought of every contingency yet, give me time. Oh, Gilly, think how much fun we'd have. Going out to a bar and dancing together. You said yourself how much you regretted we'd never gotten to dance together in public. Come on, at least give my little plan some thought, will you?"

The spectral red of Gilly's cropped hair was vivid against the backdrop of dark winter woods as at last she spoke. A little smile played at the corner of her mouth. "But we'd be in bodies. We couldn't waft anywhere. We'd need money, a car. What would we do about all that?"

"Steal," Anna said as though she had given the matter much previous attention. Seeing Gilly's puzzlement she barged ahead. "Of course, that will take a bit of planning. But the new owners leave money around all the time. More than enough for a ferry trip, cab fare, and other necessities of getting a body from place to place. If we steal it a little at a time, careful not to take too much, we'd be able to save for a trip in no time. It would be just like the fountain pen, only this time we won't put it back. What do you think?"

"Well," Gilly spoke slowly, still letting the information, the wild and wonderful plan, sink in. "Let's see now. The ferry costs about 50 cents, maybe a dollar by now. The cab shouldn't cost more than a couple of dollars. A ten spot ought to cover everything — a meal, and a few drinks included. We could probably borrow that much in a week or so."

"Atta girl. We'll have such a grand time. We'll filch the money and wait for a night like tonight when Tessa and Ellie are dead to the world. I promise never to steal another cent, but I think you and I really do deserve another chance to travel outside our boundaries and see how the world has changed. I'm so excited I could pop."

The ghosts climbed the stairs to Tessa and Ellie's bedroom and stood staring down at the low dresser.

Lying there among a set of keys, a postage stamp, and a pair of nail clippers was a crisp ten-dollar bill. "Oh my," Anna said as she tentatively reached her arm toward the dresser. Just then one of the sleeping women groaned, and Anna jerked her arm back.

Gilly laughed. "Wouldn't they be surprised to wake up and find a ten-dollar bill floating around the room. Anna, don't take it yet. They are sure to miss that much money in the morning. We should do as we planned and take small amounts." Even as she spoke the cautionary words, she felt disappointment. The adventure had become as exciting for her as for Anna, and she yearned for the taste of the world and its many pleasures. "Don't you think?"

"What I think is this," Anna said after a long and thoughtful pause. "Opportunity knocks but once. We have the funds. Our hosts are sound asleep and likely to stay that way. The house is as quiet as the proverbial mouse. I say let's get a move on."

Gilly spread herself over Ellie, and Anna did likewise with Tessa. On the count of three, they eased themselves in between the molecules of the bodies of their hosts and out to the farthest subatomic space.

"Pmmmf," said Gilly. "I must weigh a ton!"

"Lordy," Anna breathed after a moment. "I didn't remember matter being this heavy. Let's find something to wear and get out of here. I'll bet the eleven o'clock ferry will just about now be docking."

"If there still is an eleven o'clock ferry," Gilly said and hauled herself, body and spirit, from the jumble of covers on the bed.

They dressed quickly in clothing that was, on the main, either too bulky or too tight, not flowing and soft like the wide-legged gabardine slacks with pleats and side pockets they wore in the forties. But the tennis shoes they wore, which were neither canvas nor meant for tennis, were very soft and helped to cushion the blow of mortal foot to hard earth. Wrapped in heavy coats against the evening chill, they descended the stairs and stood in the moonlight-swathed living room. "Shall we?" Gilly said and opened the door.

Anna stepped into the chill night. "Let's."

The dock lay downhill from the house, so the walk to catch the huge boat wasn't all that difficult, though both felt weary from the effort of lugging bodies that far. "We'll get used to it in a while," Anna consoled as they stopped for a moment to catch a deep breath. Just then the ferry, lights ablaze, hove into view, and they hurried their pace. At the ticket counter Gilly asked for two passenger tickets to Seattle and handed over the ten-dollar bill. The bored attendant pushed the change through a small glass opening. Gilly's jaw dropped. "There must be some mistake," she said regally. "I handed you a ten."

"No mistake," the attendant said. "Two tickets, six dollars. You have four dollars coming in change."

Gilly stared at the limp bills in her hand and mentally calculated the remainder of the evening's expenditures. They still needed a taxi and cover charge. And if they wanted to eat anything or drink? "I must say prices have certainly soared since I, ah, in my absence."

"For that price, they should serve champagne," Anna said as they boarded the ferry and took seats.

Almost immediately the boat began its slow progress across the dark water to the city. Gilly laid her arm across the back of the seat behind Anna and cast her eyes around the passenger compartment. No one seemed to notice them. She let her arm fall onto Anna's shoulders and scooted closer, still looking around. The other passengers, and there were few at this time of night, either dozed or read the paper or stared out the large windows at the Sound. A smile spread over Gilly's face and another across Anna's as they sat pressed against each other, rocking and swaying with the motion of the waves.

An astonishingly short time later, the boat neared the far dock, and Gilly and Anna lined up with the others to disembark. They stepped out into the cold evening and pulled their coats tighter, lamenting again the weight of the bodies and the items necessary to keep them functioning. The bright lights and the noise and the traffic hurtling by assaulted their eyes and ears.

They stood on the dock, the last passengers left there, the wind off the water whipping their hair. Gilly was all but convinced they should turn back, but she thought again of the adventure, the daring and unheard of pleasure of seeing firsthand the goings on at the Double Barrel. She strengthened her resolve and looked to the far end of the dock, trying to spot a taxi. Grabbing Anna by the arm, she started off toward the street and a line of cabs waiting there.

Anna bent into one of the cabs and inquired

about the fare to Pioneer Square. When informed of the amount, which was more than they had left, she instructed the driver to take them as far as four dollars worth. When she attempted to enter the cab merely by wafting inside it, she bumped her head severely on the hard metal of the door. "Ouch," she said as the driver gave her a peculiar look from the front seat. Gilly reached down and opened the door, guiding Anna inside and smiling innocently at the driver.

"We'll have to be careful about doorways," she whispered to Anna in the backseat. "We can't go around tonight bumping into things. What would people think!"

"Who cares," Anna said brightly, once again thrilled with their adventure. "But one thing is for sure. They would never think they were witnessing a couple of ghosts dressed in other people's bodies, out for a night on the town."

Gilly laughed aloud and squeezed Anna's hand. "No indeed. We'll have such a grand time of it, Anna. I can't wait to get inside that place. Can you even imagine what it will be like — to see women together, as couples?"

The taxi careened through the streets in a light, misting rain, the meter clicking rapidly. The driver peered at them in his rearview mirror. "So, where you headed in the Square?"

"The Double Barrel," Anna said without even a tinge of embarrassment. "We don't know exactly where it is, though. But remember to let us out when the meter clicks to four dollars."

"You're beyond that already, and we're nowhere near the place."

"But I asked —"

"It's okay," the driver said, smiling. "I go there myself. I'll take you all the way. It's a slow night and, anyway, I like to help out family when I can." He winked at them in the mirror.

Gilly and Anna looked at each other. *Family?* Could he possibly mean what they thought he meant?

"My guy and I like to go there too. Would have been there tonight if I weren't on duty."

The revelation brought a tear to the rim of Gilly's eye. She swiped at it with her free hand while clinging to Anna with the other. *Family!* Such a safe word, so comforting. The notion that they were not alone, that they were part of a family! The idea made her head swim, but it was a wonderful swimming. The feeling of belonging, of feeling safe in the world, was like walking into a warm, firelit room filled with friends after a cold winter spent outside.

Anna snuggled closer against Gilly's warm side, her heart pounding and her palms sweating. She felt giddy with excitement. The evening was proving to be worth every risk they had taken. After tonight she would happily return to her bodiless state, loving Gilly and her afterlife just as she had done for years. But tonight, the prospect of the club and the dancing and the camaraderie made even the weighted bodies, the cold, and even the beginnings of stomach-growling hunger all seem worth it.

At last the taxi pulled to a stop at the Double Barrel. The driver gave them a smile and a wave, and Gilly and Anna stepped into the bright neon night. Mindless of the damp and the cold, they stared at the entry to the bar, gawking like kids at the clumps of people coming and going through the wide door. Women in groups or singly or two-by-two went in and exited. Men, too, in the same configurations. At one point a couple of young women exited the bar to the sidewalk where one of them drew the other to her and planted a deep, noisy kiss on her lips. They pulled apart and disappeared into the night, their pealing laughter following them into the shadows.

Inside the smoky interior, Gilly and Anna stood close together, beaming and awestruck at the panoply of sights and sounds. There was, indeed, a live band, and more astonishing yet, they were in the middle of a waltz. Couples swirled and dipped on the dance floor. A tall woman brushed past, and Gilly realized as she passed that it wasn't a woman at all, but a man dressed in women's clothing. Wide-eyed, she continued looking about the large, crowded room, her eye falling on one amazing sight before being attracted by another.

She was so caught up in the revelations that at first she scarcely noticed Anna's insistent tug at her elbow. "Gilly," Anna said in a muffled, alarmed tone. "The Swiss women. Look. Over there." She pointed to the dance floor where the Bed-and-Breakfast guests were energetically waltzing. "They'll recognize us!"

Gilly spotted the rest rooms just to the right of the dance floor and immediately steered Anna toward the door marked *Women.* They plunged as quickly as possible through the crowded tables and sped for the door but forgot to open it. Both crashed into the door and rebounded. Anna rubbed her nose, and Gilly ran her hand over her brow to soothe the bump there. "Oops. Forgot again."

Without turning to see if they had attracted any notice, they opened the door and went in. They felt silly and slightly out of place. Since neither really needed to use the facilities, Gilly made a big show of washing her hands, and Anna stood against the wall and fluffed her hair with her fingers. Several women entered and stood behind Anna in line.

One of the women, dressed entirely in black leather with chains dripping from her belt and around her neck, smiled at Anna and reached into the pocket of her vest. She extracted a small cigarette, obviously hand-rolled, and offered it to Anna with a wink. "Want a toke?"

Anna smiled and declined, announcing that she had quit smoking just after the war, but thanks anyway. The young woman gave her a peculiar look and disappeared into the stall. Vowing to be more careful about her small talk in the future, Anna stuck her head out of the door to check on the whereabouts of the Swiss visitors. They had returned to their table and were gathering their coats. She poked her head back inside to tell Gilly that they would be able to leave the loo in only a few moments.

At last they returned to the cavernous room and looked for a table. Since there were none, they opted to stand along a far wall. Dancers filled the floor, and it was a feast just to watch the couples dance and smile. A waiter approached and asked for their drink order, but neither wanted anything. The exhilaration of the music and the dancing and the evening needed no assistance from mere alcohol. They smiled at each other and at the room full of people, nodding at them as though they knew each one, as though they were all family and they had known everyone for ages.

The band finished a polka and slid easily into the next number while the dancers waited on the crowded floor. Gilly's jaw dropped. Anna froze in place. It was almost as if the band knew that Gilly and Anna were there. Chattanooga Choo Choo came tumbling and prancing out of the accordions and the guitar on stage.

In Gilly's mind, and in Anna's, the accordions were transformed into a trombone and a saxophone. A round globe of glass rotated slowly in the ceiling, casting particles of colored light over the dance floor. Gilly turned to Anna, taking her hand. "May I have this dance?"

"My pleasure," Anna replied and walked to the dance floor.

They pushed their way to the center, just in front of the band. Anna held her hands up, and Gilly clasped them. In the wink of an eye they began to jitterbug. It was done evenly, with rhythm, without so much as a whiff of effort. Gilly took Anna's arms and threw her between her legs then rolled her across her back, all in time to the music.

"I hope the next number is a slow one," Gilly said. "I can't wait to hold you close and whisper I love you while we dance to something smooth and sexy."

They danced on, mindless of the crowd, which had moved away from Gilly and Anna, leaving an ever-widening circle on the floor where only they danced. They were in thrall of each other. The crowd, smiling and snapping their fingers in time to the music, commented on how wonderfully the two young women could dance the jitterbug.

SOMEONE TO WATCH by Jaye Maiman. 272 pp. 4th Robin Miller Mystery. ISBN 1-56280-095-7 10.95

GREENER THAN GRASS by Jennifer Fulton. 208 pp. A young woman — a stranger in her bed. ISBN 1-56280-092-2 10.95

TRAVELS WITH DIANA HUNTER by Regine Sands. Erotic lesbian romp. Audio Book (2 cassettes) ISBN 1-56280-107-4 16.95

CABIN FEVER by Carol Schmidt. 256 pp. Sizzling suspense and passion. ISBN 1-56280-089-1 10.95

THERE WILL BE NO GOODBYES by Laura DeHart Young. 192 pp. Romantic love, strength, and friendship. ISBN 1-56280-103-1 10.95

FAULTLINE by Sheila Ortiz Taylor. 144 pp. Joyous comic lesbian novel. ISBN 1-56280-108-2 9.95

OPEN HOUSE by Pat Welch. 176 pp. 4th Helen Black Mystery. ISBN 1-56280-102-3 10.95

ONCE MORE WITH FEELING by Peggy J. Herring. 240 pp. Lighthearted, loving romantic adventure. ISBN 1-56280-089-2 10.95

FOREVER by Evelyn Kennedy. 224 pp. Passionate romance — love overcoming all obstacles. ISBN 1-56280-094-9 10.95

WHISPERS by Kris Bruyer. 176 pp. Romantic ghost story ISBN 1-56280-082-5 10.95

NIGHT SONGS by Penny Mickelbury. 224 pp. 2nd Gianna Maglione Mystery. ISBN 1-56280-097-3 10.95

GETTING TO THE POINT by Teresa Stores. 256 pp. Classic southern Lesbian novel. ISBN 1-56280-100-7 10.95

PAINTED MOON by Karin Kallmaker. 224 pp. Delicious Kallmaker romance. ISBN 1-56280-075-2 10.95

THE MYSTERIOUS NAIAD edited by Katherine V. Forrest & Barbara Grier. 320 pp. Love stories by Naiad Press authors. ISBN 1-56280-074-4 14.95

DAUGHTERS OF A CORAL DAWN by Katherine V. Forrest. 240 pp. Tenth Anniversay Edition. ISBN 1-56280-104-X 10.95

BODY GUARD by Claire McNab. 208 pp. 6th Carol Ashton Mystery. ISBN 1-56280-073-6 10.95

CACTUS LOVE by Lee Lynch. 192 pp. Stories by the beloved storyteller. ISBN 1-56280-071-X 9.95

SECOND GUESS by Rose Beecham. 216 pp. 2nd Amanda Valentine Mystery. ISBN 1-56280-069-8 9.95

THE SURE THING by Melissa Hartman. 208 pp. L.A. earthquake romance. ISBN 1-56280-078-7 9.95

A RAGE OF MAIDENS by Lauren Wright Douglas. 240 pp. 6th Caitlin Reece Mystery. ISBN 1-56280-068-X 10.95

TRIPLE EXPOSURE by Jackie Calhoun. 224 pp. Romantic drama involving many characters. ISBN 1-56280-067-1 9.95

UP, UP AND AWAY by Catherine Ennis. 192 pp. Delightful romance. ISBN 1-56280-065-5 9.95

PERSONAL ADS by Robbi Sommers. 176 pp. Sizzling short stories. ISBN 1-56280-059-0 9.95

FLASHPOINT by Katherine V. Forrest. 256 pp. Lesbian blockbuster! ISBN 1-56280-043-4 22.95

CROSSWORDS by Penny Sumner. 256 pp. 2nd Victoria Cross Mystery. ISBN 1-56280-064-7 9.95

SWEET CHERRY WINE by Carol Schmidt. 224 pp. A novel of suspense. ISBN 1-56280-063-9 9.95

CERTAIN SMILES by Dorothy Tell. 160 pp. Erotic short stories. ISBN 1-56280-066-3 9.95

EDITED OUT by Lisa Haddock. 224 pp. 1st Carmen Ramirez Mystery. ISBN 1-56280-077-9 9.95

WEDNESDAY NIGHTS by Camarin Grae. 288 pp. Sexy adventure. ISBN 1-56280-060-4 10.95

SMOKEY O by Celia Cohen. 176 pp. Relationships on the playing field. ISBN 1-56280-057-4 9.95

KATHLEEN O'DONALD by Penny Hayes. 256 pp. Rose and Kathleen find each other and employment in 1909 NYC. ISBN 1-56280-070-1 9.95

STAYING HOME by Elisabeth Nonas. 256 pp. Molly and Alix want a baby . . . or do they? ISBN 1-56280-076-0 10.95

TRUE LOVE by Jennifer Fulton. 240 pp. Six lesbians searching for love in all the "right" places. ISBN 1-56280-035-3 10.95

GARDENIAS WHERE THERE ARE NONE by Molleen Zanger. 176 pp. Why is Melanie inextricably drawn to the old house? ISBN 1-56280-056-6 9.95

KEEPING SECRETS by Penny Mickelbury. 208 pp. 1st Gianna Maglione Mystery. ISBN 1-56280-052-3 9.95

THE ROMANTIC NAIAD edited by Katherine V. Forrest & Barbara Grier. 336 pp. Love stories by Naiad Press authors. ISBN 1-56280-054-X 14.95

UNDER MY SKIN by Jaye Maiman. 336 pp. 3rd Robin Miller Mystery. ISBN 1-56280-049-3. 10.95

STAY TOONED by Rhonda Dicksion. 144 pp. Cartoons — 1st collection since *Lesbian Survival Manual.* ISBN 1-56280-045-0 9.95

CAR POOL by Karin Kallmaker. 272pp. Lesbians on wheels and then some! ISBN 1-56280-048-5 10.95

NOT TELLING MOTHER: STORIES FROM A LIFE by Diane Salvatore. 176 pp. Her 3rd novel. ISBN 1-56280-044-2 9.95

GOBLIN MARKET by Lauren Wright Douglas. 240pp. 5th Caitlin Reece Mystery. ISBN 1-56280-047-7 10.95

LONG GOODBYES by Nikki Baker. 256 pp. 3rd Virginia Kelly Mystery. ISBN 1-56280-042-6 9.95

FRIENDS AND LOVERS by Jackie Calhoun. 224 pp. Midwestern Lesbian lives and loves. ISBN 1-56280-041-8 10.95

THE CAT CAME BACK by Hilary Mullins. 208 pp. Highly praised Lesbian novel. ISBN 1-56280-040-X 9.95

BEHIND CLOSED DOORS by Robbi Sommers. 192 pp. Hot, erotic short stories. ISBN 1-56280-039-6 9.95

CLAIRE OF THE MOON by Nicole Conn. 192 pp. See the movie — read the book! ISBN 1-56280-038-8 10.95

SILENT HEART by Claire McNab. 192 pp. Exotic Lesbian romance. ISBN 1-56280-036-1 10.95

HAPPY ENDINGS by Kate Brandt. 272 pp. Intimate conversations with Lesbian authors. ISBN 1-56280-050-7 10.95

THE SPY IN QUESTION by Amanda Kyle Williams. 256 pp. 4th Madison McGuire Mystery. ISBN 1-56280-037-X 9.95

SAVING GRACE by Jennifer Fulton. 240 pp. Adventure and romantic entanglement. ISBN 1-56280-051-5 9.95

THE YEAR SEVEN by Molleen Zanger. 208 pp. Women surviving in a new world. ISBN 1-56280-034-5 9.95

CURIOUS WINE by Katherine V. Forrest. 176 pp. Tenth Anniversary Edition. The most popular contemporary Lesbian love story. ISBN 1-56280-053-1 10.95
Audio Book (2 cassettes) ISBN 1-56280-105-8 16.95

CHAUTAUQUA by Catherine Ennis. 192 pp. Exciting, romantic adventure. ISBN 1-56280-032-9 9.95

A PROPER BURIAL by Pat Welch. 192 pp. 3rd Helen Black Mystery. ISBN 1-56280-033-7 9.95

SILVERLAKE HEAT: A Novel of Suspense by Carol Schmidt. 240 pp. Rhonda is as hot as Laney's dreams. ISBN 1-56280-031-0 9.95

LOVE, ZENA BETH by Diane Salvatore. 224 pp. The most talked about lesbian novel of the nineties! ISBN 1-56280-030-2 10.95

A DOORYARD FULL OF FLOWERS by Isabel Miller. 160 pp. Stories incl. 2 sequels to *Patience and Sarah.* ISBN 1-56280-029-9 9.95

MURDER BY TRADITION by Katherine V. Forrest. 288 pp. 4th Kate Delafield Mystery. ISBN 1-56280-002-7 10.95

THE EROTIC NAIAD edited by Katherine V. Forrest & Barbara Grier. 224 pp. Love stories by Naiad Press authors.	ISBN 1-56280-026-4	13.95
DEAD CERTAIN by Claire McNab. 224 pp. 5th Carol Ashton Mystery.	ISBN 1-56280-027-2	9.95
CRAZY FOR LOVING by Jaye Maiman. 320 pp. 2nd Robin Miller Mystery.	ISBN 1-56280-025-6	9.95
STONEHURST by Barbara Johnson. 176 pp. Passionate regency romance.	ISBN 1-56280-024-8	10.95
INTRODUCING AMANDA VALENTINE by Rose Beecham. 256 pp. 1st Amanda Valentine Mystery.	ISBN 1-56280-021-3	9.95
UNCERTAIN COMPANIONS by Robbi Sommers. 204 pp. Steamy, erotic novel.	ISBN 1-56280-017-5	9.95
A TIGER'S HEART by Lauren W. Douglas. 240 pp. 4th Caitlin Reece Mystery.	ISBN 1-56280-018-3	9.95
PAPERBACK ROMANCE by Karin Kallmaker. 256 pp. A delicious romance.	ISBN 1-56280-019-1	9.95
MORTON RIVER VALLEY by Lee Lynch. 304 pp. Lee Lynch at her best!	ISBN 1-56280-016-7	9.95
THE LAVENDER HOUSE MURDER by Nikki Baker. 224 pp. 2nd Virginia Kelly Mystery.	ISBN 1-56280-012-4	9.95
PASSION BAY by Jennifer Fulton. 224 pp. Passionate romance, virgin beaches, tropical skies.	ISBN 1-56280-028-0	10.95
STICKS AND STONES by Jackie Calhoun. 208 pp. Contemporary lesbian lives and loves.	ISBN 1-56280-020-5	9.95
Audio Book (2 cassettes)	ISBN 1-56280-106-6	16.95
DELIA IRONFOOT by Jeane Harris. 192 pp. Adventure for Delia and Beth in the Utah mountains.	ISBN 1-56280-014-0	9.95
UNDER THE SOUTHERN CROSS by Claire McNab. 192 pp. Romantic nights Down Under.	ISBN 1-56280-011-6	9.95
GRASSY FLATS by Penny Hayes. 256 pp. Lesbian romance in the '30s.	ISBN 1-56280-010-8	9.95
A SINGULAR SPY by Amanda K. Williams. 192 pp. 3rd Madison McGuire Mystery.	ISBN 1-56280-008-6	8.95
THE END OF APRIL by Penny Sumner. 240 pp. 1st Victoria Cross Mystery.	ISBN 1-56280-007-8	8.95
HOUSTON TOWN by Deborah Powell. 208 pp. A Hollis Carpenter Mystery.	ISBN 1-56280-006-X	8.95
KISS AND TELL by Robbi Sommers. 192 pp. Scorching stories by the author of *Pleasures*.	ISBN 1-56280-005-1	10.95
STILL WATERS by Pat Welch. 208 pp. 2nd Helen Black Mystery.	ISBN 0-941483-97-5	9.95

TO LOVE AGAIN by Evelyn Kennedy. 208 pp. Wildly romantic love story. ISBN 0-941483-85-1 9.95

IN THE GAME by Nikki Baker. 192 pp. 1st Virginia Kelly Mystery. ISBN 1-56280-004-3 9.95

AVALON by Mary Jane Jones. 256 pp. A Lesbian Arthurian romance. ISBN 0-941483-96-7 9.95

STRANDED by Camarin Grae. 320 pp. Entertaining, riveting adventure. ISBN 0-941483-99-1 9.95

THE DAUGHTERS OF ARTEMIS by Lauren Wright Douglas. 240 pp. 3rd Caitlin Reece Mystery. ISBN 0-941483-95-9 9.95

CLEARWATER by Catherine Ennis. 176 pp. Romantic secrets of a small Louisiana town. ISBN 0-941483-65-7 8.95

THE HALLELUJAH MURDERS by Dorothy Tell. 176 pp. 2nd Poppy Dillworth Mystery. ISBN 0-941483-88-6 8.95

SECOND CHANCE by Jackie Calhoun. 256 pp. Contemporary Lesbian lives and loves. ISBN 0-941483-93-2 9.95

BENEDICTION by Diane Salvatore. 272 pp. Striking, contemporary romantic novel. ISBN 0-941483-90-8 9.95

BLACK IRIS by Jeane Harris. 192 pp. Caroline's hidden past . . . ISBN 0-941483-68-1 8.95

TOUCHWOOD by Karin Kallmaker. 240 pp. Loving, May/December romance. ISBN 0-941483-76-2 9.95

COP OUT by Claire McNab. 208 pp. 4th Carol Ashton Mystery. ISBN 0-941483-84-3 9.95

THE BEVERLY MALIBU by Katherine V. Forrest. 288 pp. 3rd Kate Delafield Mystery. ISBN 0-941483-48-7 10.95

THAT OLD STUDEBAKER by Lee Lynch. 272 pp. Andy's affair with Regina and her attachment to her beloved car. ISBN 0-941483-82-7 9.95

PASSION'S LEGACY by Lori Paige. 224 pp. Sarah is swept into the arms of Augusta Pym in this delightful historical romance. ISBN 0-941483-81-9 8.95

THE PROVIDENCE FILE by Amanda Kyle Williams. 256 pp. 2nd Madison McGuire Mystery. ISBN 0-941483-92-4 8.95

I LEFT MY HEART by Jaye Maiman. 320 pp. 1st Robin Miller Mystery. ISBN 0-941483-72-X 10.95

THE PRICE OF SALT by Patricia Highsmith (writing as Claire Morgan). 288 pp. Classic lesbian novel, first issued in 1952 . . . acknowledged by its author under her own, very famous, name. ISBN 1-56280-003-5 9.95

SIDE BY SIDE by Isabel Miller. 256 pp. From beloved author of *Patience and Sarah.* ISBN 0-941483-77-0 9.95

STAYING POWER: LONG TERM LESBIAN COUPLES by Susan E. Johnson. 352 pp. Joys of coupledom.	ISBN 0-941-483-75-4	14.95
SLICK by Camarin Grae. 304 pp. Exotic, erotic adventure.	ISBN 0-941483-74-6	9.95
NINTH LIFE by Lauren Wright Douglas. 256 pp. 2nd Caitlin Reece Mystery.	ISBN 0-941483-50-9	8.95
PLAYERS by Robbi Sommers. 192 pp. Sizzling, erotic novel.	ISBN 0-941483-73-8	9.95
MURDER AT RED ROOK RANCH by Dorothy Tell. 224 pp. 1st Poppy Dillworth Mystery.	ISBN 0-941483-80-0	8.95
LESBIAN SURVIVAL MANUAL by Rhonda Dicksion. 112 pp. Cartoons!	ISBN 0-941483-71-1	8.95
A ROOM FULL OF WOMEN by Elisabeth Nonas. 256 pp. Contemporary Lesbian lives.	ISBN 0-941483-69-X	9.95
THEME FOR DIVERSE INSTRUMENTS by Jane Rule. 208 pp. Powerful romantic lesbian stories.	ISBN 0-941483-63-0	8.95
CLUB 12 by Amanda Kyle Williams. 288 pp. Espionage thriller featuring a lesbian agent!	ISBN 0-941483-64-9	8.95
DEATH DOWN UNDER by Claire McNab. 240 pp. 3rd Carol Ashton Mystery.	ISBN 0-941483-39-8	9.95
MONTANA FEATHERS by Penny Hayes. 256 pp. Vivian and Elizabeth find love in frontier Montana.	ISBN 0-941483-61-4	8.95
LIFESTYLES by Jackie Calhoun. 224 pp. Contemporary Lesbian lives and loves.	ISBN 0-941483-57-6	9.95
WILDERNESS TREK by Dorothy Tell. 192 pp. Six women on vacation learning "new" skills.	ISBN 0-941483-60-6	8.95
MURDER BY THE BOOK by Pat Welch. 256 pp. 1st Helen Black Mystery.	ISBN 0-941483-59-2	9.95
THERE'S SOMETHING I'VE BEEN MEANING TO TELL YOU Ed. by Loralee MacPike. 288 pp. Gay men and lesbians coming out to their children.	ISBN 0-941483-44-4	9.95
LIFTING BELLY by Gertrude Stein. Ed. by Rebecca Mark. 104 pp. Erotic poetry.	ISBN 0-941483-51-7	10.95
AFTER THE FIRE by Jane Rule. 256 pp. Warm, human novel by this incomparable author.	ISBN 0-941483-45-2	8.95
THREE WOMEN by March Hastings. 232 pp. Golden oldie. A triangle among wealthy sophisticates.	ISBN 0-941483-43-6	8.95
PLEASURES by Robbi Sommers. 204 pp. Unprecedented eroticism.	ISBN 0-941483-49-5	8.95
EDGEWISE by Camarin Grae. 372 pp. Spellbinding adventure.	ISBN 0-941483-19-3	9.95

FATAL REUNION by Claire McNab. 224 pp. 2nd Carol Ashton Mystery.	ISBN 0-941483-40-1	10.95
IN EVERY PORT by Karin Kallmaker. 228 pp. Jessica's sexy, adventuresome travels.	ISBN 0-941483-37-7	9.95
OF LOVE AND GLORY by Evelyn Kennedy. 192 pp. Exciting WWII romance.	ISBN 0-941483-32-0	10.95
CLICKING STONES by Nancy Tyler Glenn. 288 pp. Love transcending time.	ISBN 0-941483-31-2	9.95
SOUTH OF THE LINE by Catherine Ennis. 216 pp. Civil War adventure.	ISBN 0-941483-29-0	8.95
WOMAN PLUS WOMAN by Dolores Klaich. 300 pp. Supurb Lesbian overview.	ISBN 0-941483-28-2	9.95
THE FINER GRAIN by Denise Ohio. 216 pp. Brilliant young college lesbian novel.	ISBN 0-941483-11-8	8.95
OCTOBER OBSESSION by Meredith More. Josie's rich, secret Lesbian life.	ISBN 0-941483-18-5	8.95
BEFORE STONEWALL: THE MAKING OF A GAY AND LESBIAN COMMUNITY by Andrea Weiss & Greta Schiller. 96 pp., 25 illus.	ISBN 0-941483-20-7	7.95
OSTEN'S BAY by Zenobia N. Vole. 204 pp. Sizzling adventure romance set on Bonaire.	ISBN 0-941483-15-0	8.95
LESSONS IN MURDER by Claire McNab. 216 pp. 1st Carol Ashton Mystery.	ISBN 0-941483-14-2	9.95
YELLOWTHROAT by Penny Hayes. 240 pp. Margarita, bandit, kidnaps Julia.	ISBN 0-941483-10-X	8.95
SAPPHISTRY: THE BOOK OF LESBIAN SEXUALITY by Pat Califia. 3d edition, revised. 208 pp.	ISBN 0-941483-24-X	10.95
CHERISHED LOVE by Evelyn Kennedy. 192 pp. Erotic Lesbian love story.	ISBN 0-941483-08-8	10.95
THE SECRET IN THE BIRD by Camarin Grae. 312 pp. Striking, psychological suspense novel.	ISBN 0-941483-05-3	8.95
TO THE LIGHTNING by Catherine Ennis. 208 pp. Romantic Lesbian 'Robinson Crusoe' adventure.	ISBN 0-941483-06-1	8.95
DREAMS AND SWORDS by Katherine V. Forrest. 192 pp. Romantic, erotic, imaginative stories.	ISBN 0-941483-03-7	8.95
MEMORY BOARD by Jane Rule. 336 pp. Memorable novel about an aging Lesbian couple.	ISBN 0-941483-02-9	10.95
THE ALWAYS ANONYMOUS BEAST by Lauren Wright Douglas. 224 pp. 1st Caitlin Reece Mystery.	ISBN 0-941483-04-5	8.95
THE BLACK AND WHITE OF IT by Ann Allen Shockley. 144 pp. Short stories.	ISBN 0-930044-96-7	7.95

SAY JESUS AND COME TO ME by Ann Allen Shockley. 288 pp. Contemporary romance. ISBN 0-930044-98-3 8.95

MURDER AT THE NIGHTWOOD BAR by Katherine V. Forrest. 240 pp. 2nd Kate Delafield Mystery. ISBN 0-930044-92-4 10.95

WINGED DANCER by Camarin Grae. 228 pp. Erotic Lesbian adventure story. ISBN 0-930044-88-6 8.95

PAZ by Camarin Grae. 336 pp. Romantic Lesbian adventurer with the power to change the world. ISBN 0-930044-89-4 8.95

SOUL SNATCHER by Camarin Grae. 224 pp. A puzzle, an adventure, a mystery — Lesbian romance. ISBN 0-930044-90-8 8.95

THE LOVE OF GOOD WOMEN by Isabel Miller. 224 pp. Long-awaited new novel by the author of the beloved *Patience and Sarah.* ISBN 0-930044-81-9 8.95

THE HOUSE AT PELHAM FALLS by Brenda Weathers. 240 pp. Suspenseful Lesbian ghost story. ISBN 0-930044-79-7 7.95

HOME IN YOUR HANDS by Lee Lynch. 240 pp. More stories from the author of *Old Dyke Tales.* ISBN 0-930044-80-0 7.95

PEMBROKE PARK by Michelle Martin. 256 pp. Derring-do and daring romance in Regency England. ISBN 0-930044-77-0 7.95

THE LONG TRAIL by Penny Hayes. 248 pp. Vivid adventures of two women in love in the old west. ISBN 0-930044-76-2 8.95

AN EMERGENCE OF GREEN by Katherine V. Forrest. 288 pp. Powerful novel of sexual discovery. ISBN 0-930044-69-X 10.95

THE LESBIAN PERIODICALS INDEX edited by Claire Potter. 432 pp. Author & subject index. ISBN 0-930044-74-6 12.95

DESERT OF THE HEART by Jane Rule. 224 pp. A classic; basis for the movie *Desert Hearts.* ISBN 0-930044-73-8 10.95

TORCHLIGHT TO VALHALLA by Gale Wilhelm. 128 pp. Classic novel by a great Lesbian writer. ISBN 0-930044-68-1 7.95

LESBIAN NUNS: BREAKING SILENCE edited by Rosemary Curb and Nancy Manahan. 432 pp. Unprecedented autobiographies of religious life. ISBN 0-930044-62-2 9.95

THE SWASHBUCKLER by Lee Lynch. 288 pp. Colorful novel set in Greenwich Village in the sixties. ISBN 0-930044-66-5 8.95

SEX VARIANT WOMEN IN LITERATURE by Jeannette Howard Foster. 448 pp. Literary history. ISBN 0-930044-65-7 8.95

A HOT-EYED MODERATE by Jane Rule. 252 pp. Hard-hitting essays on gay life; writing; art. ISBN 0-930044-57-6 7.95

AMATEUR CITY by Katherine V. Forrest. 224 pp. 1st Kate Delafield Mystery. ISBN 0-930044-55-X 10.95

THE SOPHIE HOROWITZ STORY by Sarah Schulman. 176 pp. Engaging novel of madcap intrigue. ISBN 0-930044-54-1 7.95